CAPTIVE
ON THE COSMAR

CAPTIVE
ON THE COSMAR

Megan Simpson

My World Books
Indiana

My World Books is a trademark of Megan Simpson

Cover photography: Jenn Reed Photography
Artwork on page *vi*: Megan Simpson

All of the Lorimerian Language in this book is typed in the Spanish Language

Summary: Robin has made a mistake. Will it take her life? Set out on an adventure with Robin as she faces marriage, death, and the high seas.

ISBN-13: 978-0615843650 (My World Books)
ISBN-10: 0615843654 (tr. pbk.)

Printed in the United States of America
Available from
Amazon.com, CreateSpace.com, and other retail outlets

Visit us on the Web:

www.MyWorldBooks.com

This book is dedicated to...
My mom, who helped me smooth out the
rough edges,
Chelsea Driver, who never turned down a
chance to read part of my book,
Daniel Schwabauer, who helped turn a pile
of ideas into a novel,
And all who pre-read my work.

vi

CONTENTS

1

GOODBYE SAINT RYAN

It was a beautiful and quiet spring morning in the sleepy port of Saint Ryan, a small bay north of the Junktivian Islands. The town was just starting to wake up and the hustle and bustle was about to begin. From a little house on the southern side of the port, an argument was brewing that would change my life forever.

"No."

"But the Mackenzie's don't mind if I go!" I insisted.

"Of course they don't, but we do." said Uncle Dallas, very sternly.

"It would be a wonderful opportunity! Just think of..."

Uncle Dallas's laughter filled the room.

"It won't cost you a penny."

"But Dear, it would cost us. You are such a huge help around the house! Think of little Zachery. He would miss you so much." Aunt Jody said.

I thought of my three cousins who couldn't miss me that much. Zachery was already 8. My 17 year old cousin, Timothy, was my best friend, but he could live without me for a few days. Kent was 19, he didn't need me, he was going to join Henry's navy. And oh, I didn't even want to think about Henry. He was the man who courted me. I prayed that Auntie would not mention him.

"The trip to Wadsworth will only take a day or two. They will stay at their grandfather's house for one short week! Besides, Toni doesn't know anybody down there. Think about how much she would miss me."

"You are being selfish and stubborn, Girl. You are only thinking of yourself!" Uncle shouted. He pounded the table with his big, meaty fist. He was very large, both in width and height, and his short brown hair was beginning to turn grey at the temples.

"Think of Henry!" put in Aunt Jody. *Oh no,* I thought, "He fancies you. It would be rude to go and leave him like that."

"This isn't about Henry. I don't even like him! And he is the one who is rude, not me. He is too old for me."

"You are 15 for pete's sake! He is only 24. He is a captain of a navy ship. Many people say he is too young!" Uncle Dallas insisted.

"He is too young for the ship, but too old for me." I could now see what they were attempting to do. They wanted to change the subject of me leaving!

"He is rich and would suit you well. Many young women would love to be in your position! He is the suitor we have chosen for you." Jody put in. Aunt Jody seemed to be the exact opposite of Uncle Dallas. She was very thin and of about average height. She had blonde, curly hair which she wore up at all times.

"But I don't want rich!" I shouted, "I don't want to marry, at least not yet. I want adventure!"

"Enough!" shouted Uncle Dallas, "I am your legal guardian. You will listen to me. You are not running away on some ship, and you are going to marry the man I choose for you. Now go to your room!"

The fight was now over, but Uncle Dallas had not won. I was going on that ship. The argument was just to see how much trouble I'd be in when I returned. I went up the stairs, and climbed the ladder into the loft where I stayed. In a small canvas bag, I packed away two of my everyday dresses. I then packed my good dress in case we went to a church service on Sunday.

I was about to close my satchel, when something caught my eye up on the shelf. I sighed and picked it up. The quiet sound of the little wind up jewelry box reached my ears. I held it to my chest and tried to remember my mother and father. Of

3

course I was only a baby when my mother passed away, and only a year old when my father gave me up to my mother's brother. I had my father's brown hair and his sea blue eyes along with his height, or so my uncle told me. I was taller than most boys and I was also left handed. Uncle didn't seem to remember who I inherited it from, but I hoped it was from my mother. I wanted to be somewhat like her.

In all of my years, all fifteen of them, I had never seen another person who was left handed. I smear my writing when I write with a quill. I can't play with the boys when it comes to arm wrestling. I can't even shake people's hands properly with my right hand.

I sighed again as I thought about how my father gave me up. I used to believe that he would return for me someday, but that couldn't possibly be true. Uncle said that he owed somebody money and had to stay hidden. That was why he dropped me off here, so that he could live without me as a burden, if he even still lived at all.

I put the jewelry box in my bag as well and hid it all under my bed. I would sneak out tonight, when nobody would notice me. I started again down the ladder and froze.

"Yes, Dear, Robin is just upstairs. I think she is in her room."

Oh no! Henry was here! I scurried back up the ladder and did something that I had started to do quite often in the past few months. I pushed back a small bookshelf and found my secret door. A few months ago I complained that a hole in the wall had let in a draft. Then I got to help Uncle Dallas replace it.

I worked from the outside; he worked from inside my room. One thing that Uncle Dallas did not catch from the inside was that I had put hinges on the outside. Late that night, I pried the nails out of place and I had myself my own secret door. Sure it sounded immature, that I was sneaking off this way, but I couldn't stand Henry.

He was snobby, cruel, and I was not going to marry him. Plus he wore one of those ridiculous looking wigs; the ones with the pony tail in the back with the hair curled on the sides. He always bragged about his hair. He said he was thinking of changing to a grey wig. I pleaded with him to not change it. He seemed to like how much I cared about his hair because he kept it the same.

I climbed through the hole and pulled the book case back into place. I sighed. I was on our neighbor's roof! I stood up from my crouching position and hurried over to where I hid the rope ladder. I pushed it over the edge and it hit the house with a soft thump. I cringed at the sound, but there was nothing to prevent it. I scurried down the ladder and into the alley as fast as possible. I ran through the alley and did not stop running. The alley let out at the meadows. I ran straight through the meadow and through the

5

woods until I came to the cliff that overlooked the harbor. That is when I stopped running and sat down.

I sat down and looked at the different ships. *I wonder which one I will be boarding.* The soft chirping from birds was all around me. *At least they are free. They are the lucky ones.* This was my thinking place, I used to love to sit here and read, or rest, or play with Timothy when I was younger. But right now, it was a good place to think, to think and to watch. I put my head down on my knees and watched the coming and going of men and ships.

I heard footsteps crunching through the grass. I looked up as Timothy sat down beside me. We sat together in silence for a while. Nobody broke the silence. Nobody wanted to. We just sat and let the world carry on.

I looked up at him and pulled a leaf out of his brown, curly hair. "You are so lucky that you get to look like both of your parents."

"Why is that a good thing?" he questioned.

"Because, I only look like my father. He betrayed me, Timothy. Who would want to look like him? I am nothing like my father."

"Don't judge him, Robin. I remember him being a good man."

"How could you remember that? You were three when he brought me to your house! He didn't want me."

Silence.

"You know," Timothy began, "I think there is a reason that you have always called my mother and father Aunt and Uncle."

"And why is that?"

"Because you still believe in seeing him again. I think that's a good thing. You shouldn't give up hope on seeing him again."

"I am going away, Timothy."

"I know." He said matter-of-factly.

I turned to face him, "You do?"

"Yes. Mother and Father know as well."

"But how could they know?"

"When I got home, Henry came down from your room holding your satchel. I tried to stop him, Robin, but he pulled the bag out of my reach and walked into the kitchen where Mother and Father were. He gave Mother the bag and she emptied it on the floor.

"She was quite startled. She demanded to know where you were and what the packed bag was for. I told her I knew where you were and that I was going to go and talk to you. And here I am."

Silence followed our conversation. It wasn't complete silence; you could still hear shouts from men down at the harbor.

"What will I do now?"

Timothy looked reluctant as he pulled something out from behind his back. "I thought you

7

would need this on your trip, so I brought it here for you."

It was my satchel!

"I repacked it for you and gave you some sweet rolls." He paused in handing the bag to me, "Promise me you will be careful and not get into trouble."

I smiled and took the bag from him, "I promise." We hugged each other for a moment. "I will be back in a week and a half. Will you take care of Zachery for me?"

He laughed, "Of course I will. If I were you, I would meet the Mackenzies at dark, so nobody else can stop you."

"Thank you, Timothy. I will miss you very much."

"Have fun, oh and watch out for pirates." he teased.

"Oh please, pirates? Are you trying to scare me out of going? Auntie told me that their age had ended."

"Father told me that *The Talon* is still on the loose, along with some of the lesser known pirates. Dillwyn is also completely overrun by pirates."

"They can't beat me!" I said, waving an invisible sword in front of me.

Timothy laughed. "Just stay safe."

We hugged again.

The sun crept closer to the horizon as I stole down to the harbor. *So far, so good.* I tried to remember the name of the ship I was sailing on. It started with an 'A'.

"Robin?" I froze in place. "Robin, is that you?"

I turned and gasped. Henry stood five feet away from me, holding his hat in place. "Robin, we are going home." I did not say a thing. I remained frozen, "Now!"

That did it. I turned and ran from him, losing him in the night crowd. I read the names on the back of the ships as I passed them. *The Charlotte, The Saint Nixon, The Pablo.* No, none of those. The last ship name was hard to read. A lamp post covered some of the golden painted letters. Ale-ndra? Oh! Toni had said that the ship shared a name with her old dog, Alexandra! This must be it. I swerved off the main cobblestone road and ducked behind a wooden crate. I watched as Henry ran straight past me.

When I could no longer see him, I stood and walked over to where the ship was anchored. It was a small ship with one mast. It was small enough to be anchored right on the port, not anchored off in the ocean farther off. I rushed up the gang plank behind someone carrying a large wooden crate over his shoulder.

Finally. I looked around, trying to spot Toni. I did not see her. *She must be below deck.*

"All ashore who goes ashore," A man beside me called out. The gang plank was pulled up and seven burley men started to hoist the anchor.

I walked to the back of the ship where I could wave goodbye to my home town. A whole week to me and Toni, how wonderful! How delightful, how... Henry?

Henry was standing ashore, jumping up and down, waving his hands and trying to flag me down. He looked concerned. "Robin!" He shouted, "What are you doing?"

I waved at him and blew him a kiss.

He looked somewhat pleased, and momentarily stunned, but then he remembered what he was doing, "Robin you're on the..." His voice was cut off by the sound of a loud horn. The ship lurched forwards. We were under way.

"Goodbye." I shouted back. I turned to start my search for Toni. I didn't know what Henry was yammering about and I didn't care.

"Robin! You're on the wrong ship!" He screamed, "You're on *The Alejandra*! Robin!"

I turned back around.

Wrong ship? What on earth was he talking about?

2

SWABBING DECKS AND
PULLING ROPES

The next day I rose early. A kind, cheerful man had offered me his bed role that I accepted. I thought it was peculiar that all of the men slept on the deck, but he didn't seem to mind. He was a short, brown haired man who introduced himself as Carlos. I had not found Toni or her family that night, but I was sure I would see her this morning.

I sat up and began to role up the man's bedroll when someone behind me began to speak.

"¡Oye! ¿Por qué ella está aqui?"

I turned and looked at the big man shouting at me. I tilted my head as he continued shouting at me in an unknown language.

"Where are the Mackenzies?" I tried to ask him.

I seemed to have angered him further because he shouted at the top of his lungs, "¡Quitarse ella de mi barca! Quitarse ella de la Alejandra!" He paused for a moment before continuing, "¡Carlos!   Dónde está Carlos?"

A man came running up from under the deck. It was the man who let me borrow his bed role.

He tipped his pointy hat before saying, "¿Qué quiere, Senor?"

"¡Carlos hay una chica en mi barco!" he said in almost a pathetic whine.

They shouted at each other in what I guessed was Lorimerian for an unknown amount of time before Carlos turned to me and said, "Hola, Chica!   Welcome to *The Alejandra*."   He sounded twice as happy as he did last night.

"The, *The Alejandra*?"

"Si, Chica!   We welcome you and we ask you, what are you doing here?"

"I, I thought this was the Alexandra, setting sail for Wadsworth."

"Ah, and there you are wrong, Chica," He said, walking to the back of the ship. I hurried to keep up with him.   "This is not *The Alexandra*, this is *The Alejandra*! Setting sail for Fernando."

"Fernando? That's the wrong direction!"

"Si, and you are on the wrong ship! Understand now?"   He inquired.   This had to be the most happy-to-be-alive person I had ever met.

"No, I don't understand.   I need to be going the other direction."

12

"Chica, the trip to Fernando will only take a fortnight! Maybe even less than! We will return to your little port in four weeks time! Isn't that wonderful?" He said with joy and pride. He seemed to be proud that their little ship could travel the Armadon in that amount of time.

"Yes. Wonderful." I slumped down against the hull of the ship.

"You know, Chica, we could drop you off at the first Junktivian Island we stop at and send you on a different ship back to Saint Ryan. Would that make you feliz? Uh, I mean happy?"

"Yes. That would make me very happy."

"Great! I need to get back to work now, Ok?"

"Yes, that will be fine." He walked down from where we stood and I followed close behind him. I decided to get a little bit of adventure out of this "vacation" so I asked him, "Is there anything I can do to help?"

"Si, Chica. There is always help to do on a ship like *The Alejandra*! You could..." He paused, looking about the ship, trying to find a job that I could accomplish, "You could mend the sails!"

"Splendid."

"Great! Go ask Ernesto, wait. That won't do. He speaks zero our language. Maybe you help Waldo in the kitchen. But he doesn't speak it either." Carlos looked greatly confused. "Chica," he said turning towards me, "I am the only senor on this ship that

13

speaks your language." Again he paused, not knowing what to do. "I know, you could help me! How does that sound, Chica?"

"Splendid!"

"Excelenté, you help me swab the deck and pull the ropes, OK?"

He pulled me over to the side of the ship where there were several buckets and mops. The stuff in the buckets smelled awful.

I helped Carlos swab the deck most of the time. On a rare occasion I helped him in the kitchen. I didn't get a chance to meet anyone, I would have if I spoke Lorimerian, but I didn't care. I was happy helping Carlos.

At long last, we docked at Dagmar Island, one of the smaller Junktivian islands. I said good bye to Carlos and started to walk down the gang plank and onto land for the first time in a whole week. I could not recall how many times I got sea sick. I lost count on my second day, but after four days went by, I could finally help Carlos to my full extent.

I started thinking of home, and then wished I did not have to leave *The Alejandra*. Carlos was a very good friend to me. During my time on that ship, he had begun to teach me some Lorimerian! I looked back up at him, watching me from the deck of the ship, and waved. He smiled and waved back. I looked forward and continued walking two steps, before I turned and ran back up to Carlos.

14

"Oh, Carlos," I cried, "I do not want to leave you!"

"But Chica," he said, taking my arm and leading me down the gang plank, "What will your parents think if you don't return to them? They would be worried sick."

A rush of pain shot through my entire body as I thought about my parents. "My parents are dead."

Carlos looked shocked, "No parents? Then why do you want to go back Saint Ryan?"

"I don't! Well I don't think I do. I don't know, Carlos. I want to stay on this ship. Just let me stay while you travel to Fernando, please!"

"Chica, believe me, you are the best friend I've had on this ship. I would love to have you for three more weeks, but I am afraid Captain Eduardo will not have a girl on the ship."

"What if," I began, looking straight into Carlos's eyes, "I wasn't a girl?"

That night, when it was dark and the men were all asleep, Carlos snuck me aboard the ship. We climbed over many snoring sailors before we could make it below deck. He lit a candle and tossed me one of his shirts, and trousers. I held the shirt up to me. Then the pants.

"These are too small, Carlos."

"Hey! I am not too small, you are too tall. Let me see if I can't find something else." He brought

15

down some other clothes. He didn't say where he had gotten them but I thought I knew the answer. I would have to have a talk with Carlos tomorrow because he slipped up the ladder before I could mention it.

I slipped off my dress, the bottom had gotten very dirty, and into the dark brown trousers. I pulled off the rest of my under skirts and put on the white shirt Carlos gave me. It was a little big, and I was lucky that I was about the same height as this man; otherwise I would have drowned in all of this clothing.

I knocked three times on the ladder, signaling that Carlos could come back down. He climbed down the ladder and looked me over three times before running back up the ladder and fetching two head scarves. One scarf was tied around my waist, making the shirt puff up a little more, and the other was used to tie up my hair. He also gave me a hat he said he bought from the tailor's store the other day.

He looked me over and sighed, "The only thing that is giving you away is your hair, Chica. It keeps coming lose."

I sighed with him and said, "We will just have to hope for the best."

Carlos went back up the ladder and asked, "You coming, Chica?"

"You know, Carlos, you will have to call me something else besides Chica tomorrow."

He smiled and said, "That I'll do, Miguel?" He finished climbing the ladder and disappeared from sight.

I waited until I could no longer hear him walking on the deck above. When I could not hear anything but snoring, I took off my head scarf and pulled out the knife Carlos had loaned me. I walked over to the bucket used to swab the deck to see my rippling, murky reflection and held my breath.

I began to chop at my hair. Fist full by fist full, my hair grew shorter. I wondered what Aunt Jody would think of me now. I also thought of Henry and the face he would make when he saw me and giggled.

My hair was now at shoulder length. I wrapped the head scarf around the top of my head and put my new hat on top. I looked at myself one last time in the bucket then gathered up the hair on the ground, blew out the candle, and climbed up the ladder. I tossed the hair scraps over board. I sneaked over to one of the barrels that lined the ship. I pried one open and grabbed an apple. *Look at me. I am a thief.* I almost put the apple back when I remembered that Carlos had probably stolen the clothes I was wearing. I slipped the apple into the scarf wrapped around me and headed over to the side of the ship.

I jumped from the ship to the dock. I did not like the idea of sneaking around, or stealing fruit, but I did not want to go back to Saint Ryan. The thought of never seeing Henry again pushed me along. Finally, a

17

life of peace, even if it meant sleeping in an ally, which was a damp and smelly place, and working long, hard days on the ship. Yes, I missed my bed. Yes, I missed Auntie's breakfasts. But no, I did not miss Henry.

3

THE JOLLY ROGER

Carlos's shocked cry woke me up the next morning. He gave me quite the tongue lashing for cutting my hair but when someone called for him from the ship, he sped up his speech.

"You remember what to say?"

"I will tell him hello and humbly ask for passage on his beautiful ship and then wait for you to talk to him."

Carlos rushed me up the gangplank and I waited patiently as he introduced me to the captain.

The captain turned and looked at me. Even though I was tall for my age, the burly man towered above me.

"Eres Miguel?"

I looked at Carlos and he nodded. "Si senor," I began. I longed to talk to him in my language, but for now, Lorimerian would have to do. I told him I would be happy to work on the ship until we reach the port of

Saint Ryan. He looked somewhat pleased with what I said, so I hoped the plan was going well.

Carlos said some more things to him, little of which I understood. The entire time, Captain Eduardo was staring me down. After Carlos finished speaking, he continued to stare at me. It looked as though he was studying me. It felt like his dark green eyes could see right through me, straight down to my little secret.

"Hola, Miguel. Bienvenido a la Alejandra!" Carlos looked pleased with whatever he said, so I smiled and nodded to him.

He started to show me around the ship, giving me a tour in Lorimerian. I had little to no idea what he said and kept looking over at Carlos. He still looked pleased so I followed the captain and when ever it sounded like he was asking me a question, I said, "Si".

I looked over at Carlos and got his attention. I pointed at the captain and then shrugged. I guess he understood me because he stopped the captain and chatted with him in his language. The captain nodded a few times before replying to Carlos.

Carlos then translated for him. "He said he is sorry for the mistake. He hopes you will enjoy your stay on *The Alejandra*."

"Welcome to my hat." The captain said proudly. Carlos flinched.

"Gracias!" I said.

He smiled at the sound of the familiar language, and then walked away quietly.

We set sail early that morning. It was great to work without everyone treating me like a child. I've caught Captain Eduardo staring at me a few times, but every time I looked up at him, he looked away. I thought he suspected something, but he didn't say anything.

The second day, Carlos gave me some lessons on how to sword fight. He showed me some positions before tossing me a sword. I caught the sword with my left hand and took up position two.

"No, no, Chica, like this." He held his sword up with his right hand and squatted down. I changed to position three and switched hands. He looked at me for a moment. "Ok, go." He swung his sword at me and hit my sword. I yelped as the sword flew out of my hand. He studied me for a moment before saying, "Switch back." I picked up my sword with my left hand. We went at it again. This time I disarmed him.

"Ah, you are a leftie!"

I looked down, embarrassed.

"No worries. I crossed blades with someone else before who was also a left hander."

On the third day after our departure, the ship seemed different, and it wasn't the thick fog surrounding us. Everyone was tense. Sailors paced back and forth along the sides of the ship.

I found Carlos standing at the back of the ship, eating an apple. "Carlos?" I asked, moving in beside him. He flinched at my arrival.

"Si, Chica?" He whispered.

"Why is everyone," I stopped and looked behind me. I lowered my voice before continuing, "Why is everyone so tense?"

"These here," he said, pointing with his apple, "Are pirate waters." I felt a shiver run through my body from my head to my toes. We stood there staring out at the misty sea. The only sound audible to me was the sound of Carlos crunching on his apple.

"Do you believe we will be attacked, Carlos?"

Carlos stopped chewing. He swallowed his mouthful of apple. "No, Chica. I have never had the nightmare of seeing the Jolly Roger, and I never will." He smiled at me and chucked his apple core into the water.

"So," he began, "You ready for more lessons?" He regained his peppy attitude, which he had lost while talking to me. "I was thinking we would work on a new…" He stopped. He leaned over the ship railing and squinted into the fog.

"Carlos?" He did not answer me. Carlos turned and ran to the mast rigging. He quickly climbed the ropes. "Carlos!" I yelled, following close behind him. "Carlos, what is it?" He did not respond. He jumped into the crows nest and grabbed the telescope from the man at watch.

Carlos gasped and dropped the telescope. It came down and the glass shattered when it smashed into the floor. "P- p- p- pirates!" He stammered. The ship below exploded with activity. Everyone rushed to the back of the ship to see what was wrong. I was the first one there with Captain Eduardo right behind me. I squinted into the mist. At first I saw nothing, but then it emerged from its grey shroud.

I don't know how to describe what I saw. To put it simply, it was pure terror. The dark brown bow of the ship seemed to shoot out of the mist. The men around me gasped, and cried out. Captain Eduardo cursed under his breath.

The ship came fully into view, and then I saw it. The Jolly Roger. It fluttered in the wind and snapped back and forth, eager for the upcoming battle. We didn't stand a chance against this three mast ship.

The captain of our ship stood at the quarter deck, shouting orders to the crew below. The men of *The Alejandra* began drawing swords and knives. One man grabbed a lantern and smashed it against the side of the ship. He and his companion grabbed shards of glass to use in the fight. Very few had guns.

The pirate ship was almost beside us. You could see the men on the ship yelling fierce war cries and jeering at us. Panels on the side of their ship opened and cannons came into view.

The first cannon fired. Its sound silenced all others. It hit the ship and the planks shattered, sending men and wood flying. Grappling hooks were thrown over the sides of our ship and a board was placed there to allow the blood thirsty men to board us.

I gasped as a hand landed on my shoulder and spun me around. It was Carlos.

"Chica! What are you doing?" When I didn't answer, he muttered under his breath and pulled me over to the far side of the ship. His hand reached up to his chest and he began to rub an amulet hanging around his neck. He kept muttering in Lorimerian as he knelt and pulled a sword out of the belt of a dead companion.

"Guard yourself well, Chica!" He tossed the sword to me then he stood, turned, and took off towards the boarding pirates, knife drawn.

The battle looked hopeless. Never in my life had I seen so much blood shed or so many deaths. I looked around, not knowing what to do.

Then a pirate dropped down from our rigging. He stayed suspended in the air with one foot wrapped around the ropes. "GARRRR!" he roared at me. I shrieked and swung my sword. It hit the ropes right above his foot. He dropped to the ground with a thud. I poked him with my sword. He moaned, but did not move.

I spun around as a large, menacing man moved in on me. His giant black beard was tangled in places, braided in others. He looked me over for a few

24

seconds. For some reason he looked confused. He shook it off and began to engage.

I took up a basic sword fighting stance. He growled at me. I swung my sword through the air. It connected with his sword with a loud twang. We continued to fight.

I rushed a cut at his left. He parried and did the same to me.

"Good! Good!" He laughed, dancing around the mast. He pressed his back against one side of the mast while I stood on the other side. He then quickly turned and hit me with the flat of his cutlass on the arm. Then he twisted the other way and jumped out from behind the pole and attacked again.

"Boy, I would like to see you when you get really mad," he taunted. I tried to hit him from above. He threw his sword up and rammed into me with his shoulder. He laughed when I tumbled to the ground. "Go on, try again. Come on, try!" He was going easy on me! This angered me and I shot up and pounded against his sword. I lunged at him and he side stepped. I fell to the floor, hitting my head in the process.

As soon as I stood up, another cannon fired and I heard a voice call, "Look out!" The mast of our ship began to tilt. The rigging holding the mast up suddenly snapped and the mast began to fall, right towards me. I started to run.

"Miss Key, No!" I heard someone call. A dark shadow appeared in the corner of my eye and a solid wall of muscle slammed into me. I slipped into unconsciousness.

4

THE KEY THIEF

My eyes opened little by little. I raised my head up, groaned, and laid it back down. My face splashed into water and I jumped to my feet. I grasped my head in pain as the blood rushed to it. I leaned against the inside of the ship's hull and tried to regain my balance.

When the headache eased, I looked around. The first thing I realized was that I was still alive. I was standing in some sort of cage in a ship's hull. Ankle deep water splashed around my feet. I did what any normal person would do; I ran to the barred door and shook it, making sure it was locked. I was alone. Where was the rest of the crew?

I began my search for a way to escape. I bashed myself against the cage sides. I tried to pick the lock. I even tried to wedge myself through two bars, but did not succeed. I sat down on a little three legged stool in despair. I perked my head up as an average height, very burly man stomped down the stairs and into view.

"Morning, Sunshine. Have a nice sleep?" He smiled at me and slid a small plate of food into my room. It floated on the water. "Eat up! Cap'n wants a word with ya." He only wore a vest and some rough looking breeches to cover his dark skin.

I was famished. I took up the plate and began stuffing my face. There was salted pork, which I devoured, an orange that did not seem too rotten, and a biscuit, which I spat out in disgust. I could have sworn that thing had worms in it. About thirty minutes later, someone new came down the stairs. It was the man with the black beard that had fought me the other day!

"Welcome," he said in a deep voice, "To *The Cosmar*."

At least I can understand them, I thought to myself. "What do you want? Why am I here? Who are you?"

The big man laughed and sat down on a bench outside my cage. "That's a lot of questions ya want me to answer. I'll start with the second one. You are here cuz I need some help on the ship. That's why I saved ya, savvy?"

"Saved me? You knocked me unconscious!"

"I knocked ya out o' the way of the fallin' mast. I saved ya cuz I thought it was kinda strange to see a Gabor like yourself on a ship with the ol'

Lorimerian flag! Now, I asked myself, why would this poor soul be on a Lorimerian ship unless he was a prisoner?"

He leaned closer to me and whispered, "You are now indebted to me. If you want to live, you better do what I ask. That way no one gets hurt."

I nodded glumly.

"Great! I think that answers number two. The third one is just as easy. I am the captain of *The Cosmar*. You may call me Captain. Understand?" I nodded again. He laughed a cruel laugh. "And now for the first one," he paused to recall what I had asked, "Ah yes, 'what do I want?' Well that one's easy enough. I want ta know your name."

"Robin." I grimaced as I said my real name. I hoped he didn't catch it.

"Welcome to *The Cosmar*, Master Robin." He bowed to me and turned to the steps. "Yo ho, yo ho a pirates life for me! Ah ha ha ha!"

Another man came down the stairs and unlocked the door. "Ya got a name?" he asked in what sounded like an Ingi accent.

"Robin," I growled.

He smiled. His face was kind underneath his chiseled features. His long dirty blonde hair was pulled back into a messy pony tail. He was about the same height as me. "Name's Kota. Captain has given me the honor of showing ya round the ship."

I smiled at him. I really needed some fresh air. We walked up the stairs and on to the deck. I squinted in the sunlight. It was a big three mast ship. The sails looked rather odd, they had wooden rods running across them horizontally.

Men from nearly every country scurried about us, some called out orders and others fulfilled them. It was hard to believe that one man could command all of these different races, all of these different thieves.

"Over here," Kota began, "Is where we all eat." He walked me over to the upraised part of the ship and took me down a few stairs into a dimly lit room. Many tables lined the floor. On one side of the small room, a counter was set up. A man stood behind the counter. "This is the mess hall. That over there is Kot. He is the ship's cook."

Kot smiled shyly at me and nodded his head.

"He was injured in a battle long ago. Lost his leg, he did. Now he wears a peg." Kota bent down and whispered in my ear, "He's a man o' few words he is. I never has heard him speak." We turned to head back up the stairs when a big man with a bigger belly slammed into me.

"Watch it, Kid." He growled. He continued to walk down the stairs. He walked over to another man, whose small, round face told everyone he was from Sakuro.

"The big one is Felix," Kota whispered. "Better stay away from him if ya know what's good for you."

I nodded. We walked back up to the main deck and Kota continued to introduce me to other sailors. "This," Kota said, pulling me over to a man tying a rope to the side of the ship, "Is my brother, Kody." I gasped when the man that turned around looked identical to Kota.

"This boy here is Robin." *Wait, did he say boy?*

"This is the new kid?"

"Aye. Captain didn't keep no one else, just him. Captain says he sees promise in him." My eyes widened. *They were all dead?*

"That I do," said a voice from behind us. Captain placed a firm hand on my shoulder. "You'll be bunking with Sasha, Master Robin." He nodded towards a little Kasimirian boy winding up some rope. Sasha looked up at the mention of his name, and then went back to work.

"Kota!" Captain barked.

"Aye, Sir?"

"Take the boy and let him help you sort through the loot. Then give him ta Felix to learn him some sword fighting."

"Aye, Captain, Sir." Kota nodded goodbye to his brother, and then we returned to the mess hall.

Felix and the Sakurian man had already begun searching through the big pile of loot. Kota said the other man's name was Yuji.

We began to rummage through the loot. Kota told me to throw anything worth something into one pile and trash into another. He also said to pull out good clothes. There were many things in the pile. I found one of my dresses and blushed at the sight of it. I buried it in the trash pile.

"Well lookie here, Boys!" Felix held up a small trinket. "It's got some gold plating on the outside."

I looked up at what he was holding and gasped. It was my parents' jewelry box!

"Give me that!" I shouted, jumping to my feet.

"Nay Boy, this one's mine."

"No, it's mine! Give it to me!" I jumped the pile of junk in a single stride. Felix stumbled to his feet and held it just above my reach.

"Robin! What has gotten into you?" Kota said, also getting to his feet.

"Can't ya tell Kota?" Yuji laughed, "He's gone pirate already!" Kota grinned, but I did not. I stomped on Felix's foot and he howled with pain. His hand dropped a little. I saw my chance and lunged for the trinket and took it from his grasp.

I dropped to my knees and slid across the floor. I opened the little box to hear the music play once more.

"Gotcha!" Felix yelled as he grabbed my shoulders. I threw myself backwards and rolled between the fat man's legs, bumping into a table leg. I was up on my feet, but I had nowhere to go. I was cornered by the kitchen counter. I set my precious box down on the counter and prepared to fight.

Felix charged me. I placed one foot against the counter behind me. When he was close enough, I pushed off of the counter and slid underneath him. I slammed into a table, sending it flying and Kota and Yuji jumping.

Felix drew his sword and charged at me again. I tried to get up, but screamed as pain shot up my leg. He raised his sword to deal the final blow, but a stronger sword stopped him.

"You know," Captain began, "To teach someone how to sword fight, your opponent needs a sword, too." He flipped his sword around so that he held the blade, and offered the handle to me. I took the sword slowly and got up.

I took up a basic sword fighting stance, or a stance similar to it since I could put little weight on my ankle, and I began to engage Felix. Felix was surprised at my strength, and so was I. I was furious. My ankle was hurt, I was on a pirate ship heading who knows where, and Carlos was probably dead. I knew what no survivors meant. They had either killed them all, or left them as shark bait.

33

I switched gears to offensive mode and pounded on his sword. When Felix stumbled and fell over a shirt from the junk pile, I turned in a full circle to build up speed and hit the hilt of his sword with my blade, right above his hand, but right under his hand guard. I twisted my sword to regain my position. In doing so, Felix dropped his sword.

It fell to the ground and clanked loudly. I stood a yard or so away from him with my mouth slightly ajar. I did not notice that all the men from the ship had gathered around our fight until they began to cheer.

Kota and Kody began to slap my back and congratulate me. They clapped. Felix stared at me resentfully. I knew I had made a very deadly enemy that day.

Kota and Kody sat me down on a bench while Yuji bandaged my ankle. When he was done, I could barely feel the pain. I nodded in gratitude.

"Master Robin," Captain shouted. The men hushed to whispers. They parted to let their captain through. He walked up to me and pulled something out of his jacket. "Well done." He tossed the trinket to me. I caught it in the air and realized that he had given me my jewelry box back.

"Thank you, Captain." Captain paused in walking. Apparently he was not used to receiving gratitude.

"Any time, young man. Now I expect every one else to get back to work, or I will make *them* fight Felix." Everyone in the room, except for the twins, drained through the single door in a matter of seconds.

I opened the box and flinched as the base fell to the floor. I held only the lid in my hands.

"No problem, Robin. Yuji can fix it." Kody tried to cheer me up. I pressed my thumbs into the middle on the fabric of the inside of the lid. It crunched. I looked at a small tear in the fabric and fingered it gently. I was surprised at how easily the stitches came undone.

"So, why exactly do you have a jewelry box again?" Kota asked me.

"Father gave it to me," I said as simply as possible. I flipped the lid around.

"Oh." He still looked confused.

I no longer paid attention to the conversation. This box didn't have any stamps or marks that said where it was from. The stitching was coming out far too easily for it to be professionally made. Unless, of course, father had made it. I kept pulling at the string until the entire corner was loose.

"What are you doing, Robin?" Kota asked.

I reached my fingers into the little pocket created by the fabric and pulled out an old piece of paper folded into a square. I unfolded the paper. It looked like a map. It must have been more than *just* a map, because Kota and Kody yelped.

35

"What is it?"

"The name!" Kota said in awe. He pointed to the corner of the map.

"Who is Victor Jackson?"

"You never heard of Black Jack?"

I remembered Kent used to say that Black Jack sailed past his old fort on the beach. He tried to scare me out of coming with him.

"He was captured last year," Kota said to his brother.

"A boat load of treasure is said to be hidden here!"

"A boat load of treasure wouldn't fit inside a treasure chest."

"He could have more than one chest!"

"Not hidden in the same place. He wouldn't risk losing all of his treasure to one person now would he?"

They threw curses at each other in different languages. Did they even know I was still there? I reached up and slide my map out of their hands.

"Should we tell Captain?" Kody asked.

"Well of course we should tell Captain ya fool!" I began to tip toe away. I turned to run.

"Blimey!" Kota yelled in surprise.

"What is it?"

"The map's gone!"

"Well blow me down! Where did it run off to?"

"You fool! Maps can't run!"

"They can if somebody stole it!"

"What do you mean?"

"I mean Robin took off with our map!"

Their yells faded away as I limped to the top deck. It was now dark out so it took me a minute to find the handle of Captain's door. I gently pushed the door open and it creaked at the effort. I found Captain sitting at a desk studying a map by candle light. His hat sat on the desk beside him, revealing his recently combed black hair. He didn't even look up as I approached him.

"Can I help you?"

"Captain Sir, I found this in my chest." I slid the map to him.

He looked at it for a moment and his expression changed from uninterested, to interested, to concerned. He looked up at me.

"Why are you giving this to me?"

"I was hoping it would make us even, Sir."

He smiled, "Who gave you this?"

"I think it was my father. It was in the box he gave me."

He looked at me as if to try and figure out who I was. He rested his chin on his hand. "Who was your father, boy?"

"Joseph Key, Sir." I said, a little uncertain.

"Well, Robin," He said leaning back in his chair, "Did you know what pirates called your father?"

"N- No, Sir."

"They called him The Key Thief. I thought the name fit well enough so it stuck."

"The what, Sir?"

"The Key Thief, and a pretty good one at that."

"You knew him, Sir?"

"Aye, I did. Did you know that he was a pirate?"

"No!" I shouted at him. "He was not a pirate! He was a merchant's man!"

Captain chuckled, "And who told ya that?"

"My aunt."

"Well she was a liar! Your father was a pirate and one of the best thieves there ever was!"

"You really knew him?"

"Aye, I knew 'im. I asked him to get me this map from Victor Jackson himself. Didn't think he ever did. He never returned. But, I guess he did get the map and he gave it to you." He opened the map and looked it over. "Hmmm, Kasper Island, I should have known," he mumbled.

"This is another reason why I saved you. You look a lot like ya dad. Plus, you are left handed. Your dad was too."

Sadness overwhelmed my heart. "Could you," I paused, "Could you tell me more about my dad?"

5

SASHA KNOWS

Footsteps could be heard outside the room. The doors burst open and the twins fell in. They were panting heavily.

"Captain, Sir!" Kota began.

"We found Black Jack's map," Kody continued.

"But Robin took it."

"And now we don't know where he went!"

"We've searched the entire ship, Sir."

"But we can't find 'im anywhere!"

"Not the entire ship," Captain said, as if their yammering wasn't unusual.

The two looked at Captain sitting in his desk chair, and then over at me, sitting in a chair to the captain's right.

"Get him!" Kody shouted.

Captain held up his hand, "Peace. He has delivered the map to me out of his own free will. We have been talking and decided to change our course now. Tell Nkunda to head east, through the Dakara pass. I will be up in a moment to tell him more."

"Uh, aye, Sir."

They exited the room and Captain continued his conversation with me. "So, Robin, who taught you how to sword fight?"

A pain much worse than a bruise or cut hit me. "It was a man on *The Alejandra*."

"And how long did he teach you?"

I tilted my head, "Why do you ask?"

"Well I want to know if you were trained, or..."

"Or just got lucky when fighting Felix?" I finished for him.

"Or if you are a natural swordsman like your father." I was shocked by what he said. "Get up," he said. We both stood and he pushed my chair into a corner. He tossed me a sword that had been hanging on the wall.

"What are you-."

"Duck," he commanded.

"What?"

"Duck!" I dropped to one knee and put the sword above my head to protect me from the oncoming sword that would have ended my life a second later.

"Get up!" he barked. I stood up and he swung his sword at me. I easily blocked the sword with a simple parry. His sword flew through the air, but I knew this was not the full extent of his blade.

I kept in defensive mode, for I did not know what he had planned, but when he nicked my leg and yelled, "Faster!" I switched into offensive mode. Our swords raced through the air. Metal clanged against metal. He spun in a circle. His sword sped through the air at head height.

I dropped to one knee and spun. Once the sword had passed harmlessly above my head, and straight into a wooden tankard sitting on his desk, I jumped to a standing position to find a sword at my neck.

"How long were you trained, Robin?" he breathed heavily.

"Nearly two weeks, Sir." He bent down and looked me in the eyes. He searched my eyes. He had a weathered face, wrinkles beside his eyes that told me he liked to laugh. His eyes were dark blue and he had bushy eyebrows. His black beard was no longer tangled; instead it was brushed and braided in spots. Gold beads hung at the ends of those braids.

"Robin," he said earnestly, "In all of my days, I have never met a man who could see the sword coming before it actually came. Not even from the top swordsmen have I seen this perfection."

I blushed and looked down at my feet.

"Robin," he continued, "How would you like to join my crew?" I was stunned.

"Me? Why me?"

"Well, because you beat one of my top swordsmen with less than two weeks of training. I saw anger and hatred in your eyes, but you did not use it."

I looked around the room, but my gaze halted on Captain's eyes.

"It wasn't me, Sir. It was Felix. He tried to use my weakness as an advantage. Then he got careless. Honest, Sir, it wasn't me."

"Well, Robin," Captain smiled, "I think I might have greater use for you after all."

That night, Captain sent me to find Sasha and get to know him before I bunked with him. I found him below deck sitting on a crate in the corner, carving something out of wood. He was humming an unknown tune when I walked in.

"Hello, Sasha," I said cheerfully. He jumped at the sound of me approaching him. The sad tune stopped and he dropped the trinket he was carving.

"Master Robin." His dark skin and thick Kasimirian accent told me where he was from. "It is a pleasure to finally meet you."

I smiled at the small boy, whose brown hair covered his purple eyes. "How do you know my name?"

"This is a ship, Sir. It is not hard to pass a rumor when there are not many people on board."

"Hmm, I guess you're right! Say, how old are you?"

"Nine and a half, Sir."

"Nine? You're only nine!"

"Nine and a half, but why does this surprise you? A lot of Cabin boys are only eight when they are sold to a ship."

"Sold? You were sold? Did your family not want you?"

"On the contrary, Sir. My family did want me. They did not have the money to keep me. They sold me to make a little extra money, but when I bring home all of the loot I have collected, we can be a family again." He seemed very sure about this. I could tell by the look on his face that he was not joking.

I sat down next to the lad. "So, Sasha," I began, "You don't suppose you could tell me something about the ship?"

"Of course I can!" His face brightened. "I know everything there is to know about this ship!"

Over the next week, all the men on board taught me very much. So much that I could not possibly remember it all. I did not know sailing was that difficult.

Exactly one week after *The Alejandra* was sunk, when it was dark and every one was asleep, I snuck above deck. I held my old dresses in my arms.

I knew I could never go back. I had grown to like life as a pirate. This had to be the missing part of my puzzle. I did not know where Kasper Island was, and I didn't care, I couldn't wait to get there.

I thought about Timothy. I thought about the day before I left. I had told Timothy that I would be back. I told him that I wouldn't get into trouble. Boy, was I ever wrong.

Yes, I would miss him. I would miss them all. But, I had a new life, a new life that I loved. The first day on board *The Cosmar* was rough. I thought I would hate life here. I thought every moment about escaping. But now that Captain had offered me a position on board the ship, to become part of their family, I could not think of a better mistake I had ever made.

I tossed the dresses overboard. They splashed quietly into the water below. I crossed my arms and leaned against the railing, thinking of my new life ahead when I heard a voice that almost sent me flying.

"What are you doing?"

"Sasha! I thought you were asleep!" I yelled as loud as I dared.

"You thought wrong." He unsheathed a small knife and held it in the air. I thought that I could probably beat Sasha in a sword fight, but when the entire ship woke up and came to his rescue, I would be doomed.

"The ship has no need of them. I thought I would lighten the load."

"Maybe you should have tossed yourself overboard too, Robin, if that is even your name."

I put my hands up in front of me, trying to calm him down, but when he turned and ran towards the captain's quarters, I pounced on him. We tumbled across the deck. I grabbed the knife from him and pointed it at him while I sat on top of him.

"You're a girl!" He breathed heavily. "Why are you pretending to be a boy?"

"You don't understand!" I shouted at him. He glared at me, but did not say a word. "You don't understand." I whispered. "Please, Sasha, please don't tell Captain or any one else. Please!"

"Why shouldn't I? Why shouldn't I go tell Captain right now?"

"Because I am sitting on top of you and you cannot run anywhere."

He wiggled beneath me. I raised the knife that had dropped slightly while talking.

"Ha! You couldn't kill me! Girls are too soft for that!" I pressed the blade against his neck and his expression changed from smug, to fearful again. "Go ahead, kill me. We will see what the Captain thinks of that! He'll have you walking the plank before the sun even rises!"

"Well then how about I throw you overboard and get rid of you now?"

His face went white.

"Fine. Can you get off of me now?" I slid off of him but held the knife up in front of him.

"Promise?"

"Promise."

I slumped down on the ship's railing. "What now?"

"What do you mean?" Sasha questioned.

"You realized I was a girl, and you are only nine!"

"Nine and a half," Sasha corrected me.

"What do I do now?"

"Well, you could find the treasure. Then share your secret. I don't think they would care if you were a girl or not if you found the treasure. They would be too happy to care."

"Sasha, that's brilliant!" I hugged the small boy from Kasimir. "Just one problem."

"I think there are many more than one problem, the fact that you're a girl would be the biggest, along with the fact that..."

"That now I have to be the first to find the treasure."

6

WALKING THE PLANK

Sasha kept true to his word. In fact, as the next week passed, we became good friends. I continued with some sword fighting lessons from Captain, now that my ankle was healed. Life seemed pretty good for me. Sasha taught me every thing I needed to know about the ship. Every time we sat and chatted with each other, I learned something new.

The lunch bell clanged just as Sasha finished telling me that the Poop deck had nothing to do with, well, poop, but more to do with religions and different languages.

"Did you know that most pirates can't swim at all?" Sasha said.

"Really? That seams a little ironic doesn't it?" I replied. *Well I know of one pirate that can swim*, I thought to myself.

Sasha laughed, but I could tell he was a little uneasy.

"I don't know about you, Sasha, but I'm starved. You want to head down to the mess hall? I overheard Kota saying that Kot was making something new and I can't wait to try it. To be honest, I've grown tired of salted pork with lime juice."

Sasha smiled. I could tell that something else was on his mind. "No thanks. Not really hungry today."

"Really? You sure?"

"Yeah, Kot gave me an extra biscuit this morning. That's all I need. Might get something later, but I am not hungry now."

I chuckled. "Suit yourself!"

I walked down into the mess hall. Today's lunch was some sort of soup. It smelled wonderful and I could not wait to try it. I sat myself down in between Kody and Kota. The smell of the soup made my mouth water. I dipped my bread into the steaming liquid and brought it to my mouth.

"Thief!" A voice cried from above deck. Felix bounded down the steps with Sasha in tow, his hands tied. "Thief!" Felix continued to yell until he had everyone's attention. Felix threw Sasha down at Captain's feet.

"This rat," he said, kicking Sasha, "Tried to take some gems from me while I was eatin'. I went below deck to fetch somethin' out o' my chest, but this thing beat me to it!"

"Calm yourself, Felix."

"Shall I ready a flogging? Or a rope for a dunking?"

"No," Captain said gently. He kneeled down to look Sasha in the eyes and placed a firm hand on his shoulder, "Is this true, lad?"

Sasha nodded his head, his sight never leaving the floor.

Captain sighed, "Then it'll be the plank for you boy."

Different cries filled the room. Some people were happy to get rid of a thief, but others, like me, tried to stop the death procession.

I was swept onto the deck. A firm hand caught my shoulder.

"Robin," Captain said roughly, "Go back below deck. This is no place for a young lady." And with that, Captain disappeared into the crowd. I stood there stunned. *What did he say?*

On deck, one of the cannons was swapped for a long board. The board was quickly tied into place by Gunter, a good and loyal friend of Felix. He happened to be the man who had fed me on my first day.

I took up a front seat right next to the plank. An idea was racing through my mind, but there were a few downsides to it. To put it simply, I was the one pirate I knew that could swim. But, with my clothes soaked and clinging to my skin, along with the possibility that my hair, which was continually growing longer, would fall out of its bun, I could be discovered. I took a quick glance at all the people crowded around the side of the ship and found Captain the farthest away from the plank. I felt pity for him. I knew that he loved Sasha like a son.

I had to save Sasha. I couldn't lose my new friend.

Sasha stumbled out onto the plank, hands still bound. He inched his way to the end of the board. He looked down at the water and then up at me. Our eyes locked. I saw the fear in his eyes.

Felix stomped on the board and Sasha fell. I watched as his helpless body flailed in the open air and splashed into the water below. That's all I had to see. I unsheathed my knife and pulled myself onto the rail using the rigging. I put the knife between my teeth and jumped. 'Man over board,' was the last thing I heard before I, along with my fears and doubts, plunged into the icy depths.

I bobbed up to the surface and searched for where Sasha was last seen. Sudden thoughts of sharks and being left behind filled my mind. I took a long breath and began my search under water. Success! I grabbed onto one of Sasha's flailing limbs and pulled him up to the surface. It was only then that I found out that I was holding him by the foot. Turning him around, I cut his bonds. When he was free, he closed his arms and legs around me like a clam. I struggled to keep above water.

A rope splashed into the water, and I tried to swim towards it. Soon there was another splash. A man bobbed to the surface. It was Captain! What did he have to do that for? Our eyes locked for a quick moment, but then I looked away. I could not save him too, and I did not want to look into another dying man's eyes. I needed to focus on saving Sasha, who was still clinging to me.

I struggled to keep above the surface. It felt as if Sasha grew heavier the longer I held him. It was only a matter of time before we began to sink. I looked up through the dark blue water and watched scenes of my life flash before my eyes. Again I thought of the promise I made with Timothy, 'Do you promise not to get into any trouble, Robin?' 'I promise'. I slowly began to close my eyes as the last bit of air escaped my lungs.

When all seemed lost, I saw a lone hand plunge into my view and grab my shirt. I gasped for air as I surfaced. Captain grabbed Sasha from me and tossed him over his left shoulder. He dragged me behind him as I tried to sort myself out.

When Captain reached the rope, he tugged on it twice and the men above began to heave us up. We were pulled onto deck. Captain ordered Yuji to fetch us some old sheets.

I am sure I looked like a drowned rat now that my once puffy clothes clung to my skin. My hat had fallen off, but my head scarf was still securely in place. I no longer worried about being discovered once Yuji gave me the old sheet that I draped around my shoulders.

When Sasha stood, Felix attempted to push him back over board, but Captain stood between them.

"Captain, Sir, he must suffer the consequences."

Captain turned and looked at Sasha, "I think the lad has suffered enough for the time being. After all, you did suggest a dunking." And with that, Felix stormed away.

Something long and wet began to slither down my back. I quickly reached behind my back and attempted to tuck my hair back into the headscarf. A hand grasped my headscarf and ripped it from my head. My hair escaped from its bun and fell to my shoulders. I stood there frozen as all eyes fell on me.

"Blimey! He's a girl!" shouted Kody, who had pulled off my head scarf.

"AHHHHHH," Yuji screamed. He fled below deck, screaming in his Sakurian language.

"What do we do with a girl?" someone asked.

"Make her walk the plank!" shouted Felix, who stood at the corner of our group.

"She can swim, what good would that do?" another shouted.

"Put 'er in the brig 'till we fig'er out what ta do with her." Gunter grunted. And that's exactly what they did. They striped me of my blanket, and I was dragged below deck and locked in the same cell as before. I sat down on the three legged stool and cried.

As the day grew old, it began to get cold. My clothes were still soaked and I had no extra covering; I shivered and hunched into a corner. I heard footsteps coming down the wooden stairs. Captain came into view. I lowered my head in humiliation. He unlocked my door and allowed me out.

"The crew says I shouldn't come and see you." Captain winked and sat down on a crate. "They decided your punishment." I turned away from him. "They said you should be left down here for three days. No food, no water, no one to talk to." He paused and looked over at me. "What do you say?"

"How did you know?" came the reply of my muffled voice.

Now it was Captain's turn to be embarrassed. He looked away from me and I caught a glimpse of guilt in his eyes.

"Perhaps I should tell you a short story. Your father," he began, "Asked me of a favor. He asked me this before every mission I sent him on." He looked up at me, "He told me that he had a child, a daughter. He asked me to watch over you if he failed his mission. After I sent him to fetch Black Jack's map, and he didn't return, I went to search for you where your father told me you would be. You were not there. I thought I was too late, that you had crawled off and drowned yourself in the river. I thought you were dead.

"I am a pirate. I could not trade my crew in exchange for the time it would take to search for you. I am sorry I did not find you sooner."

I looked up at him. He did not make eye contact with me, and when he did, he looked away. I stood up, "You're lying." I said plainly.

He looked at me and then smiled and sighed. "Yes, I am. I did find you, Robin. I found you. You were at the dock house right where your father said you would be. But I could not take you with me."

"Why not? You don't understand how long I waited for a real life to fall upon me!"

"I could not take you, because you were not ready."

I froze. "Not ready? How was I not ready?"

"You were only a baby! A baby who could not survive without a mother. That is why I took you to your aunt's house."

"You took me? I thought Father dropped me off and ran."

"He loved you Robin." A tear formed in my eye. I turned around to look at him. He became interested with something on the floor and did not look up at me when I approached. He flinched as I hugged him. "Come," he said standing up.

"Where are we going?"

"I need to make a little announcement." I followed him up on deck.

"Captain!" barked Felix, "What are you doing? She's supposed to be down there three days, not thirty minutes!"

"I believe I've changed my mind, Felix." And with that, we walked away. He took me up by the tiller of the ship, right above the captain's quarters, and stopped behind the railing that separated us from all of the rest of the crew.

"Listen up!" Captain called to the crew below, "This here is Robin Key, daughter of Joseph Key." whispers spread through the ship as I stood beside Captain.

Captain reached inside his big, dirty black coat and pulled out a small charm. He pulled it off of his neck and tied it around mine.

"She is one of us now." Silence. Then Kody stood up on an upturned bucket and began to clap, slow at first, and then faster. Kota joined in, and then Sasha followed. Soon every one but Felix, Gunter, and Yuji, who had developed a fear of girls on boats, applauded. I stood in front of them. Captain put his hand on my shoulder and then left. I turned to go, but looked down at the cold stone charm around my neck. I picked up the charm and held it in my hands. It was a skull and crossbones, the symbol of the pirates. The charm was made of jade, and was streaked with red. I fingered the beautiful Ruby that was laid inside the stone and let the conversation with Captain fill my mind.

7

THE GREAT RESCUE STORY

The Cosmar doesn't even compare to The Alejandra. On The Alejandra I was mistreated, even when I was dressed like a boy. But on The Cosmar, I was family, and I prospered. My friendship with Sasha grew. I excelled in sword fighting lessons. I learned everything I needed to know about ships and sailing. It was a pirate's life for me.

One day, while Sasha and I swabbed the deck, he educated me about the ship.

"So this is a Junk?" I asked him as I dipped my mop into the smelly bucket.

"Yup!"

"Why haven't I heard of these before?"

"Not much of them around any more." He paused for a moment, "Didn't anyone ever tell you the origin of the name of the Junktivian Islands? Named after a boat like this, they were." Sasha was interrupted by a call from the crows nest.

"Ship approaches!" We all ran to the side of the ship to try and spot the sailing vessel. A Gabor flag flew above the blue ship.

The ship came closer and closer. We could nearly make out the faces of the men.

"Ahoy, merchant ship, have you no flag?" a slick voice called from the other ship. The voice sounded familiar, but I could not put my finger on it.

"We are from here and there, but nay, we fly no colors."

"Explain your purpose here in these waters, and we will let you pass by peacefully."

"Are you threatening me my good man?" Captain asked, toying with the man from the blue ship.

"Nay Sir, but if you don't tell me your purpose, or what flag your ship flies, we'll have to board you."

"Prepare for boarding," Captain whispered to Nkunda, the first mate, "I don't want them to know that we are pirates, we have too few crew members."

"Aye, Sir," Nkunda answered. He walked down the stairs, calling out orders to everyone he passed, "Hide the Jolly Roger, hide the guns and swords! We are not a pirate ship! We are a merchant ship! Prepare for boarding!" He continued calling to us. My good old friend, fear, began to creep into my mind again.

Captain continued to yell at the other man who was speaking, trying to persuade him from boarding our ship.

"Tell us the name of the ship you are sailing." called the familiar voice.

"I'll tell you ours if you tell me yours." Captain replied simply.

The other man paused, "You are playing us, Sir, perhaps stalling? I can assure you, my good man, that we mean you no harm. We are searching for someone, a girl. Goes by the name..."

"Now, my dear captain, I believe you are stalling! Tell us the name of your vessel and we will tell you our purpose!"

"Very well. My ship is called *The Vengeance*!"

I gasped and ran to Captain, "Sir! Did he say the name of that ship was *The Vengeance*?"

"Aye, I believe he did."

I finished climbing the stairs, "Captain Sir, I know this man."

Captain seemed surprised. "Really? Who is it?"

"Henry Jones, Sir, Captain of *The Vengeance*. Sir, this man is dangerous! He is the youngest man ever known to command a ship like that, Sir. He is highly trusted by the King of Gabor. I suggest avoiding boarding if at all possible."

"I am afraid it is too late for that," Captain said, looking at the approaching vessel, "We do not have enough men to fight." Then Captain called to Henry, "I have been informed that you are Henry Jones. What do you want? My vessel is under way and we would hate for a delay."

"It seems that you know who I am, but I do not know who you are." He paused, waiting for an answer, and when none came, he continued. "Very well. We are searching for a girl round the age of sixteen. She boarded a ship named, *The Alejandra*. Do you know of this ship?"

Captain seemed very annoyed. "Aye, I know of it. I happen to know that it is at the bottom of the Armadon Sea!"

"You lie, Sir! We found several men set adrift who claim to be part of the crew of *The Alejandra*!" *There were survivors?* "They said they knew of no girl, but one man claims that he knew Robin, and told us she disguised herself as a boy to gain passage on the ship." Carlos was the only one who knew, Carlos must be alive! "Prepare for boarding and we will not draw weapons!"

"I hope this is not a threat, for I have armed men of my own! Leave us! We have no further business with you." That did it. Grappling hooks flew over the side of our ship. The ships thumped together and a board was placed on the railings.

Henry led a group of five men onboard our ship. I averted my eyes from him and made way for Captain's quarters.

"Robin!" Someone called. I did not have time to see who it was. I ducked inside Captain's room. I rushed to hide behind his desk when something caught my eyes. Black Jack's map was unrolled on the desk! If Henry saw that, he would know that we were pirates! I quickly rolled up the map and hid it within the belt of my pants.

Shouts filled the air outside the cabin, and I dared to take a peak. Outside, a man from *The Vengeance* held the Jolly Roger!

"Well, it seems we have discovered your little secret." Two of Henry's men drew their swords and pointed them at Captain. Three men pointed swords at the other two. Soon all swords were drawn and pointed as someone else.

"Filthy pirates! Did you really think you could hide from me?" Henry sneered. All the men from *The Cosmar* pointed drawn swords, or cocked pistols at Henry. Henry's men soon ignored Captain, who had not moved since they boarded, and pointed them at the men from *The Cosmar*. All of the swords and pistols soon returned to their original position.

I ran into the middle of the crowd. "Stop!" I yelled. All swords lowered slightly. Henry turned to see what the disturbance was and gasped when he saw me.

"Robin?" He asked. He looked as if he had seen a ghost.

"There is no need for blood shed, Henry. Take me and leave them alone." I turned and looked Captain in the eyes. "I will be all right," I whispered.

"Robin?" Henry asked again. I nodded. "Oh, Robin, it is you!" He hugged me and lifted me off my feet. "What on earth are you wearing, my beloved?" I nearly threw up in disgust.

"Men, disarm! We'll take Robin and leave them to rot!" All at once the men sheathed their swords and left our ship. Sadly, I left with them. The last glance I got from our ship before being taken into Henry's quarters, was of Sasha, mouth slightly ajar, holding out his hand as if reaching for me.

Henry said he had to take care of some things concerning the crew and that I was allowed to roam about the ship. Several of the men on board I recognized as friends of Henry's. All of them looked rough. They were tall and several had huge battle wounds across their arms, torso, or face. I was glad Captain decided not to fight them for I am afraid that the battle's outcome would not have been pleasant.

There was one man that I was particularly pleased to 'run into'.

I was on my way to find Henry when I turned and bumped into someone carrying a crate. The man dropped the crate and it burst open, its contents spilled onto the ground.

"Oh, I am so sorry, Sir!" I apologized. I bent down and began to pick up apples and oranges from the ground.   Soon, only one apple remained.   I reached for it and placed my hand on it. His hand settled on top of mine.   I withdrew my hand and looked at the man who I knocked over.

"Kent?" I asked, my heart rate increasing.

"Robin?"

"Oh, Kent, it's you!"   I hugged my cousin tightly.

"Timothy was right!   He did see you on that filthy pirate ship!"

"Timothy is here?"

"Oh, he's around somewhere.   I bet you are so relieved to be rescued."

"Well... Oh, that doesn't matter!   I have had the best adventure you could ever imagine!"

"But you were stuck on that awful pirate ship and good heavens!   What are you wearing?"

"Have no fear, Kent; I have a dress for her below deck."   Henry intruded.   "If you don't mind, Kent, I will be taking Robin now.   Tell the first mate to make way back to Saint Ryan."

"Yes, Sir!"   Kent picked up the last fruit and scurried off.

"Henry, did you say that there were survivors from *The Alejandra*?"

"Hmm? Ah, yes. Six awful smelling men were falling out of a cutter when we found them. They're about somewhere... Now come, let's get you dressed."

Henry gave me a beautiful gown to wear. It matched the ship I was on, big, blue, and expensive. It was only when I slipped into the itchy dress and tripped over the hem of the skirt that I missed the shirt and trousers I had worn.

Henry brought me into his quarters and shut the door. He offered me a chair and I accepted it. He took his seat opposite of me. I looked around the grand room. Henry's wealth was obvious. Several golden statues sat in corners. Paintings and old swords hung on the wall. My gaze swept across the room and landed on Henry. He leaned back in his chair, hands locked behind his head, his left foot sitting on his right knee.

"You look absolutely gorgeous in the dress I bought for you! How are you, my flower?"

I turned away, embarrassed, "Fine I guess."

"Only fine? Well, I guess if I were in your position I would be a little shaken too!"

"In my position?" I said, raising my voice slightly.

"Yes. A poor girl kidnapped by ruthless pirates. A great rescue story if you ask me!"

"A great rescue story?"

"Yes! Can't you see it? Captain Henry Jones saves his betrothed from ruthless pirates!"

"Those 'Ruthless Pirates', were my friends!"

Henry gasped. "Oh look at what they did to you!" I tensed, feeling the adrenaline begin to rush to my arms and legs, "They cut your hair!"

I relaxed slightly.

"So, how are Aunt Jody and Uncle Dallas doing? You know, with me gone?"

"Hmm? Oh yes, um, not sure really. You see I came looking for you with Kent and, ah, your other cousin. I did not have time to check on them. I was so worried about you, Robin."

I was mad now. Henry claimed to be the best man I will ever know, and yet he couldn't remember Timothy's name or take the time to check on my aunt and uncle!

Henry must have seen the tension growing inside me, because he asked, "Are you feeling all right? You look sick."

"Fine! I am fine!" I said through gritted teeth.

"Oh good. I wanted to ask you something but didn't want you to faint."

"Ask me what?" I said, standing up.

"A very important question."

I backed up against the wall.

"Robin, will you m-."

"No!"

"But I-."

"No! A thousand times no, Henry! Don't ask again because my answer will always be no!"

"Look at what those pirates did to you. They drove you mad, Robin! Come back to me. We are family."

"No!" I screamed at him, "Those 'Filthy Pirates', those 'Nasty Sea Rats', those 'Monsters', are my family. You can never, ever, ever replace them!"

Henry's chest puffed out, he stood tall. "I don't know what they did to you, Robin, but know this. I will get you back. I will rescue you from where those filthy pirates drove you. I saved you from them. I saved your life!"

"You didn't save my life, you stole it, and I want it back!"

I reached behind me and drew the sword from the wall hanging. Henry flinched. "I will not fight you, Robin."

"Then you will die a coward's death," I yelled and lunged at him. He side stepped away. I tripped on the hem of my skirt and crashed to the ground.

When I sat up, Kent came running through the door, waving something in the air. "Henry! Look what I've found in Robin's trousers!" He gave it to Henry. His facial expression was a mixture of excitement, confusion, and anger. One of those emotions was caused by me, lying on the floor. The first was probably because he had uncovered something of great value. This was obvious because of the smirk on his face. And the last, well, was because I was the one he took the map from.

"Steven!" Henry called out. A man, who appeared to be waiting for us, walked through the door. He was of average height, thin, and had dirty brown hair pulled back into a neat pony tail. His green eyes seemed to glow in the dimly lit room.

"It's Robert, Sir."

"I don't care! Take her and lock her in the brig. This isn't the girl whom I spoke of." He stared at me as he said, "This is someone else."

Robert began to drag me outside. Just as we reached the door, Kent spoke up, "No, I am pretty sure that's Robin, although I have no idea why she was on the floor."

"Oh, shut up, you fool!" Henry shouted as the door slammed shut.

Henry had me bound and taken below deck. I held my chin up. Henry was not going to beat me. I was going to escape; I just had no idea how. I did not make it easy on the poor sailor that had to drag me below deck. I squirmed and pulled and tugged. He took me down two flights of stairs to the bottom of the ship. He led me into a barred room.

"My name is Robert." I averted my eyes from him. "I don't mean to be rude, ma'am, but I heard your conversation with the captain. You are the one he is looking for, aren't you?"

"No! Henry wants someone else. Someone who will obey his every wish. Someone that's not me."

"Sorry miss, didn't mean to intrude." Robert then began to pour some water into a dish. "I don't know what you did to him, but I have not seen him this mad before and trust me, I've worked on this ship for three years, I know what Henry's anger is like."

I smiled downward, looking at the floor. He unsheathed a knife and reached towards my hands. I jerked them away, my smile quickly turning into a scowl as I stared at him. He held his hands up and slowly reached towards mine once again. He slipped the knife under the rope and cut it. The rope fell to the floor.

"I will be back tomorrow." And with that, he left.

The next day, Henry visited me. His anger seemed to have calmed the slightest bit, but I was sure it wouldn't last for long.

"So, have you changed your mind, Robin?"

"It depends. What was my mind set on?"

Henry chuckled, but did not smile. Maybe it's better to say that he grunted.

"Robin, I gave you a new life. Any girl would want to be in your position, why not you?"

"You did not give me a new life, you destroyed my old one."

"Robin, if you are saying that you prefer the pirates then I..."

"That's exactly what I am saying. For a while I thought you were deaf."

"Listen, Robin, if you don't want to marry me, if you want to be adventurous and play pirates, then I will play along as well!" He turned to the man who had a huge scar from a burn wrapped around his wrist, "You!"

The man stood at attention, "Yes, Sir!"

"No food or water today. We will see if that changes her mind. And I want my dress back!" The other man smirked, and with that, both left. A while after they had gone, Robert came and visited me again. He gave me a drink from his water canister and an apple to eat. He also gave me a change of clothes.

"Henry threw your old clothes overboard, so this is all we have for you." He passed a Gabor uniform to me. He left the room while I changed into some itchy off-white color trousers. A long sleeve, puffy shirt that was slit open slightly by the neck followed. I then put on a thick red wool jacket with white trim. I shouted to Robert and he reentered the room.

"Henry is playing a cruel game. Trust me when I say that I would rather be on your side," Robert joked.

"Then why aren't you on our side? Why don't you want to be a pirate?"

"I was kidding, Robin."

"Were you? Were you really?" Robert stood there shocked. "You can still be a pirate, Robert." Robert began to look frustrated.

"No! I have sworn my allegiance to the King of Gabor; I can not take it back now."

"Take the King's Pardon! Many men do it."

"Apparently women do too." Now it was my turn to be angry.

"I didn't have to take anyone's pardon! I chose to be a pirate out of my own free will!"

"Good for you."

"Robert it's not t-."

"No, it is too late! Robin, it's hopeless. To join you now would be asking Henry for a death sentence."

"I did."

"And look at you now." He paced back and forth in front of my door. "I tried to help you, Robin, but by doing so, you have shown me my wrongs. I can no longer assist you."

"Thank you."

"What?"

"Thank you for what you have done so far. Thank you for cutting my ropes, thank you for feeding me and giving me a drink. Thank you for letting me talk to you. Thank you."

He looked shocked and confused. "You're, um, you're welcome." He turned to leave.

"Wait! Could you send Timothy down? I have not seen him since I boarded."

"Henry did not tell you?" He said, looking over his shoulder.

"Tell me what?" I said, standing up from the wooden bench. Robert sighed.

He turned to face me again, "Your cousin, Timothy," He said very slowly, "Has been reported missing." And with that, he turned and ran up the stairs.

8

THE COST OF FREEDOM

Thunder boomed and the ship rolled from side to side. I shivered in the darkness. The hard damp floor that I slept on did not help. Once Robert decided to stop lending help and torches, time seemed endless. In the dark of night, you couldn't see your hand in front of your face. Now I had nothing but my Gabor coat to keep me warm.

Discomfort was the least of my worries though. I fingered the little pirate charm that hung around my neck and thought about *The Cosmar*. I could not get Sasha's dreadful face out of my head, the day that Henry took me. I thought of all the crew. I couldn't imagine them trying to reach the island without a map. I didn't know what they would do now.

But the thing that bothered me most of all, was that Timothy was missing. I wondered if he was taken captive by Captain, or if he fought against them and died, or if he was somehow thrown overboard. I couldn't imagine him joining us, and I didn't have time to think about it now. My morning meal was being carried down the stairs.

Henry had decided that he was 'Too Kind' to let me starve down here so he declared that I would get one meal per day. Louis, the burned first mate, brought me my single meal today. I so missed Kot's amazing cooking compared to the food I was given on *The Vengeance*. I was given salted pork, a hard biscuit, some sort of fruit, and unidentifiable mush. I longed to be back on *The Cosmar*.

Thunder boomed again and I wrapped myself tighter in my coat. I perked my head up at the sound of shouting. I moved my little chair over to the side of the ship. I stood on it and peeked out of the tiny hole in the wood. *What was that sound?* I thought as something boomed not too far away. *That couldn't be thunder...* My eye widened as I saw what was heading my way. I dove to the floor just as the cannon ball slammed into the side of the ship. I screamed and covered my head as fragments of wood flew around me. Water gushed into the hole the cannonball made. I heard the distant sound of sword fighting and hopped to my feet.

Heavy footsteps could be heard coming down the stairs. The water now covered the floor. Louis approached, sword drawn. A huge gash was spread out across his shoulder. He seemed weary. He took out his keys and began to unlock the cell door, his eyes never leaving mine. I turned around and looked for a weapon. I picked up the bench I had been sitting on.

I turned back to the man. He smiled a nasty smile as the key creaked in the lock. The man lurched forward against the cell door. I stepped to the right. Sticking out of his chest was the blade of a sword. The bald man fell to his knees as Robert pulled his sword out of him.

"Robert!" I called out to him. He dragged the dead sailor out of the way of the door.

"The ship is under attack, Robin. I believe your friends missed you." I smiled as he came over and continued to unlock the door. A fierce war cry came from the second floor and a man of Henry's tumbled down the stairs, dead. Kota bounded down the stairs and leaped over him. He looked at me, then at Robert. For some reason, killing Robert was more important than saving me, so he engaged Robert. Robert backed away from the door to defend himself from Kota.

The water now covered the top of my feet and was steadily increasing. I reached through the bars and twisted the key all the way around. The lock clinked and the creaky door swung open.

"Robin!" called Kota, "Get out of here! Someone is waiting for you on the second floor." I hesitated before running up the stairs. Both of these men were on the same team, and yet they didn't know it. When both swords were separated, I jumped in between the two.

"Stop it, stop it! Kota, he is on our side. He has been helping me." The two lowered their swords slightly, their gaze never leaving each other. "Robert, this is Kota." I placed my hand on Robert's sword hand and pushed it down. "Kota, Robert." And I did the same thing to him. "Now, can we get off of this ship?"

Thunder boomed again. Kota smiled and walked through the ankle deep water over to the man Robert killed. He groped around in the bloody water for a second, and then he pulled a cutlass from Louis's belt and tossed it to me. Surprised, I caught it in the air.

"You want me to fight with you?"

"Why else would we come and rescue you, Robin?" I grinned and we walked to the stairs. At the bottom I stopped and grabbed Kota's shoulder. "Sorry I took the map."

He raised an eyebrow, "You don't need to apologize to me."

"That's what I am afraid of."

"Well apology accepted. Honestly, girl, if we didn't forgive you, do you think we would be here saving you right now?" We continued up the stairs. "And besides, Sasha would not even let us think about leaving you behind. Oh and by the way," he stopped me half way up the stairs. "Is he really..."

"Robin!" I turned to see who yelled my name and nearly dropped dead.

"Timothy!" We ran and embraced each other.

"I thought you were dead." Timothy choked. Tears filled his brown eyes.

"Oh, Timothy, it is so good to see you again."

We hugged for a moment longer then Timothy suddenly grabbed my shoulders and pushed me away. "You little lair!"

"What?" I was shocked by his change in attitude.

"You said you wouldn't be gone long. How long has it been? Three weeks?"

I looked down at the ground, "Five." I mumbled. Timothy sighed. Then he smiled. "What are you grinning about?" I asked him. He thumped me on the shoulder, "Ow!" I yelped.

"Honestly, Robin. I don't know if I should hit you again, or tell you happy birthday!"

"What?"

"Happy sixteenth birthday, Robin." The month had slipped by so fast. I guess it really was my birthday.

"But, Timothy, why did you join the pirates?"

He seemed uneasy, "I didn't mean to at first. I saw you from *The Vengeance*. I called out to you, but you kept running. I snuck aboard your ship, *The Cosmar*, to look for you. But you weren't there. I searched below the deck and when I returned to the top, our ship had left me stranded on a pirate ship. At first I was held hostage, but then once I revealed who I was, the captain seemed to take pity on me and made me part of his crew.

"It was spectacular, Robin. No rules, a fairly easy life, well, easier life than on *The Vengeance*, and it was only a matter of time before you and Kent boarded the right ship."

"You want Kent to come too?" I asked excitedly.

"Of course, he is my brother after all."

"Hey! Come on you two, I can't tell who is winning from down here!" Kota called. Robert peeked his head out of the hatch, and then ducked as a sword flew above his head.

We parted and drew our swords together. The four of us charged to the upper deck. Lightning streaked the sky as we went above deck. The fight faired well for *The Cosmar*, although Henry was nowhere to be seen. I wondered if he was dead or worse, hiding.

I ran straight through the door to Henry's room. I searched high and low for the map. It wasn't in there, which meant Henry couldn't be dead. He was hiding, and he had the map. I ran back out to the deck and began searching for Captain to tell him about the map.

I engaged a bald man with a pointy beard near the bow of the ship. He was fast, but I was faster.

Before he could even get into position, I sliced across his arm. A deep cut formed. I hit the hilt of his sword and twisted, just like what I did to Felix. His sword flew from his grasp. I planted my heel into Baldy's chest, knocked him off of his feet and sent him backwards. I pounced on him and held my blade to his throat. He closed his eyes, completely giving up, even though he could have overpowered me right there. I readied myself for the kill, but I couldn't do it. I could not kill an unarmed man.

"You owe me," I whispered in his ear. I jumped off of him and fled before he even opened his eyes.

A blood curdling yell pierced the air. This single scream of pain stood out above all others. I stood locked in place. I dared to turn around, slowly of course. My limbs did not seem to cooperate with me.

The rain made it hard to see, but there, right beside the wheel, stood Henry and Timothy. Both swords were drawn, except Timothy's was lowered, nearly touching the ground, and Henry's sword had been plunged into Timothy's middle.

I screamed for him. I began to run towards him. The world seemed to go in slow motion. The edges of my vision grew dark as I pushed my way through battling, sweaty men toward Henry and Timothy. I tried to force my legs to go faster, but I was stuck in this slow moving horror.

Once I reached them, Timothy had fallen to the ground and Henry cleaned his sword on a handkerchief.

"What have you done?" I screamed at him. "You've killed him! You killed my cousin!" I could not contain the tears any longer. They spilled over my cheeks.

I drew my sword and pointed it at Henry. He laughed. "Robin, you've tried fighting me. You ended up a heap on my floor! I will not fight you, Robin."

"And I will not marry you! I would rather die than marry a monster like you." I saw the wrath and hatred growing in Henry's eyes.

"If I can't have you, then no one will! I will not have a peasant girl reject me, Captain Henry Jones!" He drew his sword and we fought. Henry first seemed surprised by my skill with the sword, and then annoyed. The fight went downhill after that.

I slipped on a puddle of water, mixed with blood, and lost my balance. Henry took advantage of this and spun in a full circle. Helpless, I raised my sword above me. His sword met mine with a strange twang, and then my sword broke in half, both parts flying out of my hand.

Thunder boomed yet again and Henry stood up tall. He reached towards me and grasped his hand around my neck. I tugged on his hand, trying to release the ever growing pressure. My feet lifted off the ground and I hung helpless in his grasp. My vision started to blur and go fuzzy.

"Last chance, Robin. This is your last chance."

"No!" I said and attempted a yelp at the pain my answer brought.

"Then you will die, arrg!" He yelped. He dropped me and I flailed around, landing one hit on his jaw and another on his leg before I slammed onto the ground. I gasped for breath, forcing air through my throat and into my lungs.

I looked up at my rescuer. My vision blurred and I swayed. I could see a short man with his hands wrapped around the hilt of a small dagger, the blade of which was sticking into Henry's thigh. It was Sasha! Henry swatted Sasha away like he was no more than a bug. He flew through the air and tumbled down the stairs, landing in a motionless heap at the bottom.

I tried to yell to him, yet nothing came from my throat, but a squeak. Henry plucked the dagger from his thigh and threw it on the ground. He looked at me and smiled a blood filled smile. As he walked towards me, another figure jumped in front of him, sliding across the wet floor, he engaged Henry. The captain of The Vengeance fought against the captain of The Cosmar. Even though Henry was injured, he was beating Captain. If Captain couldn't beat Henry, then I knew I couldn't.

Timothy screamed, arching his back. His arms were wrapped around his middle, so I could not see if the wound was serious.   I grabbed his foot and began dragging him towards the stairs.   He flailed around. He must not have seen me.

"Timothy, it's me, Rob..."   His other foot landed a kick to my jaw and I tumbled down the stairs. I sat there, dazed, before I realized that Sasha was limp beside me. I tried to stand, but my mind was still foggy. I grabbed Sasha and inched my way toward the gangplank. Someone reached down and grabbed Sasha from me. I struggled for a moment and then looked up at who it was. Nkunda beckoned for help. A man rushed over and Nkunda raised his sword. They said something, but I looked at Sasha, who began to stir.

"Help," I whispered. Nkunda looked down at me, and then back up at the man. He nodded his head and the man reached down for me. I was lifted up into the air and carried over the gangplank. Kota and Kody dragged Timothy across after us. Captain came last, fending off four men at once to cover our escape. The ropes were cut and another cannon was fired from *The Cosmar*.

The ships started separating. The gangplank splashed into the water. Captain dove over the railing and caught onto the rigging. I was taken below deck. I did not remember what happened after that.

9

LAND HO

We lost Henry in the storm and continued on our journey. The mess hall was used to house the few injured men that we had. Only two men had been killed in the fighting on *The Vengeance*, and only one man might not survive his injuries. That man was Timothy. I had not been allowed in to see him yet, but my hopes raised as Captain walked over to me.

"Your cousin wishes to speak with..." I jumped up and raced to the mess hall before Captain could finish speaking. I ran into the dimly lit room. Tables had been pushed together making seven makeshift beds. I found Timothy at the very back of the room.

"Oh, Timothy!" I cried. I could barely look at him. His shirt had been removed and changed into bandages which were wrapped tightly around his middle. Even though the wound had been given hours ago, blood still soaked the bandages. His head was propped up on a pillow, his face a ghastly shade of white.

"Robin!" He said somewhat excitedly. He tried to sit up but all that came from that was a coughing fit. Nkunda raced over to us. He made Timothy swallow an awful looking purple liquid before making him lay down again.

Kot joined us in our little huddle over Timothy.

"Robin," Nkunda said in his strange accent, "We need change bandages again. I suggest you leave for moment."

"I can't leave him, not now. He needs me."

"Robin," Timothy whispered. He turned his face away from me, as if embarrassed. "I... I can't stand... you seeing me... like this." He wheezed, "Please go."

I was trying to hold back tears, but now I let them flow freely.

"Perhaps you could be use to us." Nkunda said. "Robin, bandages need washed in kitchen. Bucket filled with water on floor. Bandages on counter. Wash and hang up to dry. Then you come back to Timothy."

I sniffed and wiped away some fresh tears. "Anything I can do to help." I walked calmly to the kitchen counter and grabbed the bandages. I took them inside the small room used for cooking and was surprised by how clean and bright it looked compared to the mess hall. The walls weren't the same dark wood as the rest of the ship. Many candles glowed brightly from the walls. As soon as everyone was out of sight, I dropped to my knees and began scrubbing furiously at the cloth in the icy cold water. I wrung them out and hung them up to dry as fast as I could. It took a total of three minutes to wash all of the bandages.

I started walking back to Timothy's bed, but stopped when I saw what was going on. Captain, Kot, and Robert were all holding Timothy down while Nkunda applied a strange liquid substance to his wound. Timothy cried out and arched his back when the medicine dripped into the open wound. He tried to wiggle out of their grasp, but he was no match for the three muscular men.

I nearly threw up at the sight of his wound. Blood covered his torso. A deep hole in his chest was the cause of the bleeding. Around the edges of his wound was an ugly shade of green. I turned from the men. I tried to make myself useful by helping the other hurt men. I thought I recognized a man from The Alejandra, but I couldn't tell for sure. I sat down next to him and gave him a long drink of water, which he took gratefully.

I stopped helping and straightened my back when I heard people whispering behind me. I strained my ears to hear more...

"What we do? We tell her?" The strange voice belonged to Nkunda.

"Of course we tell her. She must know." Captains calm voice said.

"Agreed, we tell her." replied Robert.

"But, who will tell her?" came a high, squeaky voice. I could not even guess who said that.

I jumped as Captain placed his hand on my shoulder. "Robin."

"Captain, Sir!" I stood up at attention.

"Robin, I, um, I have something to tell you." I looked up into his dark blue eyes. I immediately knew what had happened. I stood there, stunned.

"No. No! He is not dead. Don't you lie to me, Captain, Timothy is not dead!" I grabbed the water bucket sitting beside me and took off for the kitchen. I tripped on a board jutting out from the floor and fell. I sat up just to catch the water from the bucket in my lap. I took the over turned bucket from the floor and raced to the kitchen.

Captain met me in there. I was scrubbing at a bandage, trying to get the stains off of it. Timothy was not dead. He couldn't be. I refused to let myself believe that Timothy was dead. I took the wet bandages and hung them up on the counter to dry. I looked up and nearly fainted. I had to grab onto the counter to keep myself from falling over.

Kody and Kota held a long board that looked to be the plank. A motionless figure lay on the board, covered with a light blue blanket. Captain motioned for me to come with him. On wobbly legs, I followed them up the stairs and over to the side of the ship. There, they dumped the figure over board.

Long after Kody and Kota left, long after everyone gave their condolences, long after Timothy was gone, I stood there. Captain brought me out a blanket and offered it to me. I did not say a word. Instead, I looked out at the endless blue ocean, at the setting sun. Captain draped the blanket over my shoulders and walked away.

After about two hours of standing there, watching the sun set, someone walked up behind me. A hand rested on my shoulder... "I'm sorry about your cousin, Chica."

"Carlos?" I spun around. "What are you doing here?"

"I carried you over from *The Vengeance*."

"That was you?"

"Aye, Chica," he embraced me in a hug. "I have missed you, Chica. I had feared for the worse when we didn't find you in the wreckage."

"What exactly happened when I left? I thought you all died!"

"I saw your captain carrying you away onto his ship. They sunk us all right, but that didn't mean we didn't survive."

"I am just glad you did survived."

There was an uncomfortable silence that followed. "I am sorry about your cousin, but I know how you feel better! Do you have something to remember him by?"

"That's a great idea." Without saying another word, I rushed below deck. I tore open my satchel that had been spared from *The Alejandra*. Nothing, nothing, nothing! I had nothing to remember Timothy by.

I barely noticed when Sasha walked down the stairs, holding a small wooden box in his left hand, since he had broken his right wrist trying to save me.

"Robin?"

"Not now Sasha."

"But I ha..."

"Not now!"

"But Captain..."

"Sasha! Can't you leave me alone! Not now, ok? Just go! Go away!" Sasha opened his mouth to say something then stopped. He closed his mouth and clenched his jaw. Tears formed in his eyes, but I turned away from him.

"Fine!" He turned to leave but stopped and turned back. "Have you even thought about how this affected others, not just you? Timothy was my friend too. But I guess you are too blind to see it. Don't ever speak to me again!"

He threw the box against the wall and it shattered. "Sasha, wait." I insisted.

"No!" He turned and ran to the steps. With tears in his eyes, he said, "I wish we left you on *The Vengeance*." And he disappeared up the steps.

I was stunned by his anger and stayed under deck for a while. Soon, I got hungry and went above deck. Items from the ship were pulled into a circle on the deck. A brightly glowing lantern that lit the night sky sat alone in the middle of the quiet circle. Men sat on crates, on barrels, and on an old rolled up sail. They ate their food silently. I grabbed a plate from the bench beside the mess hall stairs and looked for a place to sit.

I saw Sasha sitting on a long crate just opposite of me and I went to sit by him. Sasha looked away from me as I sat down beside him.

"So, what were you going to..." I stopped talking when Sasha got up and sat on the rolled up sail. I looked down at my food. Kody and Kota jumped in beside me, one on my right and one on my left.

"Happy Birthday, Robin! How ya been, Robin?" Kota asked cheerfully.

"Ya! How ya been?"

I got up and walked over to the food crate. I handed Kot my still full plate. He whimpered slightly. "Sorry Kot, I'm not hungry anymore, even if it is my birthday." I took off for the stairs leading below deck when somebody jumped in front of me.

"Watch where you're going," I yelled at him and tried to continue on my way. He stepped in front of me again. I looked up at the man blocking my way. It was Captain.

"Robin, can I have a word?"

I wiped a tear from the corner of my eye. "I guess."

Captain led me to his cabin and closed the door behind us. He sat down in his big chair behind his desk. I sat down in a smaller chair opposite of him. "Will you be okay?"

"Eventually." I looked away from him, "Sorry I took the map."

Captain laughed a big, hearty laugh that filled the room. He must have seen my confusion because he asked, "Why are ya apologizing to me?"

"Because we don't have a heading!"

"Who said that?"

"I, um, just thought that..."

"Thought that we needed a map to have a heading?"

"Exactly!"

"Oh, Robin, not having a map just adds to the adventure. We know what Black Jack's secret mark is, the one that leads us on the trail. We will be fine." He winked at me. I smiled for the first time that day. I looked at the big map spread out on the table. I blinked. I looked more closely at the map.

"Captain?"

"Yes, Robin?"

"What is this?" I asked, pointing to little marks on the map that said "M.F.""J.T." and "T.M"

"Those are the initials of all that we buried at sea. That there," he said, tapping the "T.M." "That's your cousin."

"What?"

"We mark all burials at sea."

A warm feeling rushed through me, chasing out the cold I had felt all that day. A long, peaceful silence followed. I was the first to break it.

"Captain?"

"Hmm?"

"Can I ask you a question?"

"Knowing you, I believe you are going to ask more than one."

I smiled again, "What is your name?"

The old sea man seemed taken aback. He smiled down at the table through his black beard. He looked around me at the door before saying, "My name is Bartholomew Smith. And I want to let you know, that this is the first time I have revealed to anyone my name in about seventeen years."

"Who was the last person you told?" I asked, resting my elbows on the table and my chin on my hands.

"Your father."

"Oh." My smile faded.

"Any other questions?"

"Um, yes."

"And?"

"Well, why is this ship called *The Cosmar*, and what does it mean? I was just wondering what this ship's story was."

"That's a very deep question, Robin. It will take time to answer." I scooted my chair closer. Captain laughed. "Very well, many years ago, this ship was a slave ship in the Junktivian Islands. It carried slaves to Laron."

"That's not far from Saint Ryan!"

"Yes. Well, they had just picked up some new sailors at Sakuro and were heading towards Dagmar when it happened." He paused, trying to remember the story.

"When what happened?" I urged him forward.

"Mutiny."

"Mutiny!""

"Aye, mutiny, and a mighty fine one too. My grandfather was there. He was a new recruit along with Nkunda.

"Nkunda was there!?"

"Aye, he was the ships cabin boy."

"Where is Nkunda from?"

"Nobody knows. Some say he is from far up north where the sea is frozen every time of year. Not many people travel up that way because no food grows there. Nobody knows the secrets of the Lonely Tribe on surviving the cold, harsh weathers of the Icy North."

"I always took Nkunda as an odd one."

"Yes." He looked lost in his thoughts. "Let us get back to the story. My grandfather hated the slave trade so he joined the crew of the *Night Stalker*."

"So he hated the slave trade, and then he joined it? That does not make any sense to me, Captain."

His deep, booming laugh filled the room again. "No it doesn't, does it? You see, he planned the mutiny. The mutiny was a success. They pulled the ship into a trading post at Dagmar Island and killed every slave trader there. The native people of Dagmar Island were afraid of the well known ship, so afraid that they ran and hid from the people on it. My grandfather decided to call the ship *The Cosmar*, which means Nightmare in their native language.

"The ship passed on to my father, and when he died, on to me. I'm not really sure when it became a pirate ship, but I am guessing Grandfather kept attacking slave ships and got the name 'Pirate' slapped on to it."

"Wow, I bet no other ship has a story as grand as this."

"Not many ships have a story at all. Any more questions, Girl? It's getting late."

"Just one. I heard... a voice last night. When I was helping with the hurt, and..." I stopped, not sure if I should continue.

"And what?"

"Well, I couldn't picture who it belonged to."

"What did the voice sound like?"

"It was kind of high and squeaky and;" I did not finish what I was saying, for a man swept into the room.

"Dinner is served, Sir!" said the same squeaky voice. I spun around in my chair to look at who the voice belonged to. There, holding a tray of food and bowing was Kot. He straightened his back and his gaze rested on me. His eyes blew up wide in surprise. He did not say a word; he just stood there like a statue.

"That would be Kot." said Captain cheerfully. Kot continued to stand there, frozen in place, so Captain turned to me and said, "Robin, why don't you join the men outside. I think I hear music if my ears are not mistaken."

"Yes, Sir. Thank you, Sir." I stood up and walked towards the door. "Sorry, Kot," I said as I passed him. I patted him on the arm as I left the room.

Music and laughter filled the night sky when I exited Captain's room. Kota stood on a rather tall crate and held a fiddle and Carlos stood on a lower crate next to him, playing on a mandolin. They played a happy tune while the rest of the men danced and sang.

"Yo ho, yo ho a pirates life for me!" The men sang in unison.

Then one man broke off into the next verse, "We swindle and plunder and rifle and loot,"

"Drink up me hardies, yo ho!" sang another. I laughed as two men, holding tankards, linked arms and danced around the lantern, their drinks splashing out of their cups.

"We kidnap and burn and don't give a hoot,"

"Drink up me hardies, yo ho!"

A muffled voice came from the crows nest. The music stopped and everyone looked up.

"Call it again, Bengt!" Kota called up to the unseen man.

"Land ho!" came the quiet reply.

Cheers erupted on the ship. Glasses were raised and toasts were made. Laughter and music soon filled the night sky once more. "Yo ho, yo ho, a pirates life for me! Yo ho, yo ho, a pirates life for me!"

10

KASPER ISLAND

The men rose earlier than the sun the next morning to prepare the ship for landing. Much still had to be done. I managed to catch a glimpse of the island before Captain called us all into line. The island was beautiful! It felt so good see another color besides blue on the horizon. Green, leafy trees rested on golden sand. A large mountain rose from the heart. After we were lined up, Captain chose five men to accompany him to Kasper Island. I was among the chosen along with Robert, Bengt, Carlos, and Peter, who was an excellent tracker.

We all loaded into the longboat and the boat was lowered into the water. Captain and I sat at the front of the boat, out of the way of the other men who rowed us to shore. We all jumped out of the boat once we reached shallow enough water. Robert and Bengt pushed the boat up onto the sand while the rest of us stopped to gaze at the beautiful trees swaying above us.

"So!" Said Robert cheerfully as he joined us on the beach, "What are we waiting for?"

"A heading." Captain said. "We walk around the tree line until we find it."

"Find what?" Robert asked me as we started walking.

"Black Jack's mark."

"Oh, well as long as it's obvious."

I laughed as we headed toward the tree line.

There it was, carved into a palm tree. The mark of Black Jack. A "B" and a "J" were carved into the tree. Three long claw marks stretched across it. I thought it was curious that the trail was not hidden, but nobody else seemed to notice.

"Is that the mark?" Robert asked me.

"Aye, that's it. It's the same as his flag." Captain said.

"What's it mean?"

"It means we are on the right path." He explained. "Peter!"

"Aye, Sir?"

"You and Bengt may lead."

They drew their swords and made their way to the front of the group. Leading with their swords, we entered into the jungle. I was surprised at how easy the trail was. You would think that a treasure like this would be more concealed. An awful thought occurred to me and I raced up to Captain.

"Yes, Robin?"

"I was just..." Fear shot across my face as I saw what lay ahead. I ran as fast as my legs could carry me to the front of the line.

"I don't know what the problem is," Bengt was saying to Peter, "There is no sign of danger anywhere." Then he took one more step and began to fall into a pit filled with deadly spikes. He began to scream. He continued to scream. He kept screaming even though I had grabbed onto the back of his shirt and pulled him to safety. Even once he was seated firmly on the ground, he kept screaming.

"Shut him up!" Captain called as he covered his ears. "The entire island is going to know we are here!"

I squatted down in front of him and slapped him squarely across the face. He was stunned for a moment, then he opened his mouth to scream again, but I stopped him by covering his mouth with my hand.

"Bengt! Stop screaming! You are ok!" I removed my hand, cautious that at any moment he would continue his screaming. When no scream came, I stood up and looked down into the hole.

"Help the man up, lad." Captain motioned to Carlos. Captain looked to the left and then to the right. "Which way, Peter?"

"You might want to wait a second, Cap." I said, holding onto a tree branch while looking over into the death trap, "I believe you might want to see this."

Captain walked over to me and peeked into the trap. A man lay down there, pierced by at lest five of the deadly spikes pointing upward. Captain muttered under his breath.

"That's one of Henry's men." I said. I felt light headed and thought it best to step away from the hole.

"Peter, which way."

Peter kneeled to the ground and ran his hand over the dust. "Men went that way."

"Excellent, then we will..."

"Wait," he turned.

"Yes?" Captain asked, looking impatient.

"They came back," He looked up to the left, "And went that way."

Captain nodded his head towards the path that swerved off to the left, "Onward."

Robert thumped me on the back as we continued on the trail. We passed another trap, this one consisting of two logs that would have swung together and smashed us when we tripped the wire. The trap had already been sprung though, and another of Henry's men was rolled over to the side. We went under the two swinging logs and continued on our way. Captain decided it best if we kept quiet, thinking we'd best not let Henry know that we were here.

We came to an old rickety bridge stretched out over some falls. Peter lead us, followed by Bengt, then me, and then Captain and Robert. We left Carlos stationed behind us to help us back across if need be. Suddenly, a plank snapped beneath the weight of Robert and he fell. He caught onto the bridge with one arm and the bridge lurched to the side. Peter jumped the rest of the distance across the bridge. Bengt followed him although the plank he landed on also snapped and he was stuck with one leg through the bridge.

I fell to my knees, along with Captain. I looked around. There! Hanging over the falls was a palm tree with some of its roots sticking out over the edge. It wasn't very big, but it would have to do. I braced myself and then dove over the rope railing and caught onto the trunk. Captain cried out when the tree started to bend, but that was what I had planned. I swung my legs over the branch to crawl backwards to Robert.

I let go with my hands and hung by my knees. "Robert!" I called out to him. He looked up and reached towards me. Our hands locked. He let go of the bridge and the tree bent even further. I swung him towards the cliff. His foot caught the edge, but he fell and swung back. I swung him again and he caught onto the tree with his leg. He wrapped both legs around the tree and let go of my arm. He began to shimmy backwards toward land. I followed. The tree groaned. Dirt fell from the roots that were over hanging the water fall.

Peter grabbed Robert's shoulder and twisted him up so that he sat on top of the tree. Then he helped him back up the rest of the way. I could hear the roots snapping. The tree pitched and fell. It jerked to a stop as the vines holding it snapped tight. I screamed as my legs fell loose from the tree. One vine broke and the tree tipped. The vine recoiled and hit my left hand, making me let go. I now hung on with only my right hand.

I swung my arm up. It hit the branch, but slid off, making it rain bark on top of me. I swung again, but ended with the same result. I began to swing, forwards, then backwards forwards, then backwards. Another vine broke. I let go and flew towards the cliff. My hands and feet grabbed nothing but dirt that poured down on top of me. I scrambled for a hand hold but found nothing.

I began to slide down. I lashed out with my hand and caught onto something. The tree fell over top of me and I flattened myself against the cliff wall. My hand slipped and I let go, but I did not fall. I looked up and saw Captain hanging over top of me. He pulled me up the rest of the way and I sat, stunned, by the edge of the falls. We all sat in silence.

A twig snapped in the distance and we all jumped to our senses. Looking closely into the depths of the jungle, I could just make out Henry's men.

"Captain."

"What, Peter?"

"Look."

Annoyed, Captain turned to look at Peter. He was pointing to the dirt. Captain turned around and studied the ground.

"How many people, Peter?" Captain asked, looking at the footprints.

"I would say fifteen at the most."

"Back," Captain said urgently.

"What?" I asked him.

"Back to the beach!"

"But why? We have come this far already and it would just be..." Bengt began.

"That's why!" Captain shouted, pointing a finger towards Henry's men. Shouts erupted. The men turned around and started running back down the trail. "They must have heard the tree falling. I told Nkunda to go ashore and find a good spot to make camp. It should be nearly ready by now. If only we can get there fast enough..." His voice trailed off as we started running back down the path.

Robert and I led the way. We crossed the bridge with little trouble, and ducked under the smashing logs. Soon we reached the death trap. Robert kept running straight past the correct path so I had to grab hold of his shirt and pull him in the right direction. I waited by the pit for the others to catch up while Robert scouted ahead.

Captain rounded the corner next, followed by Carlos and Peter, and then Bengt. When Bengt reached the trap, he slowed his pace to a walk. I grabbed his arm and dragged him the rest of the way to the beach.

Captain and the others in our group waited for us at the beach. They were looking off into the distance. I joined them to see what they were so focused on and realized that it was Henry's ship.

"How on earth could we have missed that?" I asked.

"It was easy," Robert said, "We were looking for the mark, not a ship."

I walked across the beach to get a better look at it when I saw something drawn in the sand. "Captain!" I called him over to me.

"You called me over to show me a footprint?" He asked. In the sand was a crudely drawn map! With a footprint in the middle...

"Captain, this is the map, I would recognize it anywhere!" I said while tracing the paths with my finger.

"Where are we?"

"Umm," I said while studying the map, "Right here, by the mark of Black Jack."

"Nkunda will have parchment. We can copy the map then. Where do you think we have made camp?"

"I have a hunch," I said, pointing to the toe of the footprint. Half concealed, was a name, -bonero Fort.

"Bonero Fort?"

"Fort Kabonero, Sir. I believe we will find our men there." I told Captain. "But I also think we will find Henry's men here. His ship is right there," I made a new dot in the sand, "Right next to Fort Zarr." I pointed again.

"Well, Robin, if we weren't in such of a panic, I think I might just make you our new navigator," Captain said, proudly.

"No time, Mr. Captain, Sir." Carlos said as he struggled to help Robert move a fairly large rock close to the map, to block the wind from messing it up. We then made our way to Fort Kabonero.

My guess was correct. Most of the men had been moved to the fort, which was half on the beach, half in the jungle. The fort was, of course abandoned and we made sure to stay clear of several buildings that looked like they would fall in the coming storm. Other than that, the fort had secure walls with four watch towers. One of the gateway doors had fallen off of its ancient hinges, so some of the men were placing logs with sharpened points firmly in the ground by the open space. Robert joined them while Captain handed out jobs to everyone.

"Robin, I am putting you in charge of the fort. I want us ready for an emergency. We have too few men as it is so I don't want to risk a surprise attack." He put several other men in charge of things like scouting, transporting stuff from the ship to Kabonero, and finding fresh water. Captain then left to draw the map.

When he returned, he called me over to the side.

"Robin."

"Aye, Sir?"

"The men will need food by morning. We do not have much left on the ship. I believe there are some fruit trees along the north wall. If you do not mind fetching some..."

"No problem for me, Sir."

"Find Nkunda and ask for a basket. I've put him in charge of inventory."

"Aye, Sir."

Nkunda was in a building along the south wall. Crates and barrels were being dropped off or rolled to him. He then told whoever was carrying the cargo where to put it.

"Nkunda!" I called to him.

"Ah, Robin! What can I get for the little missy?"

"Something to carry food in. Perhaps a basket, or a bowl, or a... turtle shell?" I asked as he set a giant shell in my arms.

"All we got. Go now, have to feed filthy sea rats something."

I left and headed for the gate. I found the trees right where Captain said they would be. The fruit I could not identify I put in a pile close to the fort wall while the other fruit I recognized went into the turtle shell. Some of them were so rotten that when you picked them up, they disintegrated into a slimy juice. Others were piles of unidentifiable mush.

I pulled some of the better looking fruit, which I did not recognize, out of their pile and placed them on top of my growing pile to show to Nkunda. Then I hefted my turtle shell, and hauled it back to Nkunda.

Nkunda was still in the hut ordering people where to put crates. I showed him the fruit I didn't know.

"Nope, nope, yes, definitely not, probably, and oh, oh no, not this one!" He said while sorting through the fruit. He then started sorting through the pile I thought was safe to eat.

"Don't worry about those. I know them by name," I said, proudly.

"What about this one?" he asked me, holding a red fruit that looked to me like a dried apple.

"Apple, of course! There weren't many of them though."

He held it by what looked like the stem to me and dangled it in the air. He then shook it. Two giant claws popped out of what I had thought was a fruit, followed by the other five legs, one of which Nkunda was holding. I shrieked as he dropped the creature and watched curiously as it scuttled out of the room.

"I'd say a crab apple."

"Yes," I said, still in shock, "Better check the rest then too."

"Bring back all fruit of this kind," he said, holding up a brown fuzzy fruit.

"Uh, ok." I said. He threw the fruit to me as I walked out of the door, turtle shell in tow.

"Oh, wait, Robin!"

I peeked my head back into the room, "Yes?"

He jogged over to me with something wrapped in a sheet in his hands. "Captain wants to give to ya." He said while unwrapping the object. He then dropped the sheet and revealed a sword and sheath. The case itself was enough to make my jaw drop. It was black with silver vines wrapping its way down from the top.

He handed it to me and I gently pulled the handle to free the blade from its sheath. The handle was black and inlaid with silver. The hand guard was also of silver. I gasped when I saw that the blade itself was a light shade of red. "I, I, well, um, thank you!" I stuttered.

"Captain found out on beach. Cleaned it up. Thought you could use sword that doesn't break. Use it well, Robin. You are the best sword woman I ever seen."

"How many sword women have you met?"

"Well, oh not the point. Good luck, Robin."

"Thank you, Sir." I left the room, twirling the sword in my hand. I dropped my shell and began to fight an imaginary opponent. I did not notice Carlos coming up behind me until I nearly killed him. I swung my sword in a full circle.

"Hey!" Carlos shouted as he ducked. He grabbed my sword arm to silence the blade.

"I'm so sorry, Carlos!"

"No worries, Chica, where ya heading?"

"There are some fruit trees on the northern wall. I am heading there now."

"Oh," he said, looking disappointed, "I thought you might want to train with me some. I haven't had to use my sword since the pirate attack."

"Maybe after I am finished we can train?"

"Sounds great! I guess I will work at the front gate then."

"It will only be a second. I will meet you there." I left in a rush. The sooner the fruit was collected, the sooner I could use my new sword. I ran straight through the gate, and straight into Captain. We both fell to the ground with a grunt.

"Captain, Sir, I am so sorry!" I said, getting up off of him.

He laughed as he pulled himself up to his feet and brushed the sand off of his black coat.

"I take it you got your sword?" he asked me, still chuckling.

"Aye, Sir, and it's just brilliant!"

"That's good, Robin, now run along."

I watched his happy face change into one of concern. "What is it, Captain?"

He sighed, "I hoped you wouldn't get involved with this, but I sent scouts out to see where Henry made camp. His men left the trail this afternoon and made way for an old bridge across the river. Only one scout came back."

My expression changed quickly.

"We have to attack by tonight."

"Why?" I asked him, confused.

"Because of high tide. When the water rises in the ocean, the river becomes too high to cross except by that single bridge that Henry has guarded."

"Well then why don't we wait until tomorrow to attack?"

"Because, Robin, we don't have enough food for another day. We barely have enough food for today."

"But the fruit I..."

"The fruit you collected is already eaten."

I raised my eyebrows in surprise, "But, I was in there nearly three minutes ago! How on earth could it have been eaten already?"

"We have nearly twenty five men on shore and you collected twenty fruit. The men are still hungry."

"Well then I better get the rest."

"Good luck, Robin, and be careful."

I ran to the northern side of the wall. I held the brown, fuzzy fruit up to each pile to try and find its match. Confused, when I did not find its match the first time, I looked more carefully. The pile wasn't there! It was gone!

"Robert?" I called out, thinking that he had played a trick on me, "Bengt? Kota, Kody? Peter?" I paused before adding, "Sasha?" I unsheathed my new sword and let it lead me into the forest. "Hello? Is any one there? Hello," I called into the dense jungle. I lowered my sword, thinking that one of the other men must have come, recognized the fruit and taken it to Nkunda.

A twig snapped behind me and I spun around. My eyes became wide with surprise. I raised my sword up and pointed it at the wild looking man. His clothes hung from his thin frame and he had really shaggy hair. His dark deep eyes just added to his creepy demeanor. And what finished off this strange man was the old, rusty sword he was pointing at me.

"Who are you and what do you want?" I asked, placing both hands on my sword and rising it up to what I hoped was a threatening position.

He chuckled and said with a deep and scratchy voice, "Go."

I kept my sword raised and did not move.

"Go home, little girl."

My heart was trying to pound its way out of my chest as I tried to think of what to do. He moved his sword closer to mine and ran its rusty blade down mine, and then back up, making an awful noise that I hoped someone heard. I decided to take a defensive position incase he attacked.

"Bad choice," he said once he realized that I was not going anywhere. He attacked so quickly, I had barely enough time to raise my sword in a simple block. He kept me in retreat for quite a while.

I then came to my senses and fought back. I had a plan that I knew his rusty old sword could not withstand. Instead of trying to hit the man, I aimed the edge of my sword at the center of his. It hit with a clang and the blade snapped in two. It flew off a ways and landed sticking up in the sand. Again I held my sword pointed at him. He breathed heavily with his half sword lowered at his side.

I opened my mouth to question him, but he hit my sword with what was left of his and it flew from my grip. Now it was my turn to be stunned. His sword lowered again and he grinned with victory.

Not giving him time to raise his sword, I pounced on him, knocking him over. I stomped on his half blade, pinning it, along with his hand, into the sand. I then placed my foot on his chest, and grinned down at his dirty face.

His face went blank. His dark eyes seemed to lighten and grow wider. His jaw dropped slightly.

"Robin?" he asked.

My eyebrows met in a frown. "Who are you?"

"Robin?" he asked again.

"What do you want?"

"Robin?"

I pressed harder on his chest with my boot, "Who are you!" I screamed at him. When he did not respond, I commanded him to drop his weapon, which he did instantly. I kicked it and it flew a distance before landing in the sand, causing a small dust cloud to rise. I ran to pick up my sword, and when I looked back he was standing, sword in hand.

"Oh, please tell me," He said, dropping his sword and falling to his knees, "Who are you?"

I clenched my jaw and pointed my sword at him. "My name is Robin Key. Who are you?" I was shocked when the poorly dressed man grabbed onto my leg and began sobbing. "Get off!" I said, shaking him off of my leg. "Give me one reason why I should not kill you now."

He smiled at me and then stood. "I," he began, "Am Joseph Key." I gasped and nearly dropped my sword.

"Who are you really?"

"I am your father."

"No, my father's dead."

"Not dead, but long forgotten." He said, taking a step towards me. I took a step back and he looked defeated.

"Proof," I said, "Give me proof."

"Joseph?" said a voice from behind me.

The man, who claimed to be my father, straightened his back and looked past me.

"Barty?"

"Joseph, is it really you?"

"Oh, Barty!" He said, running to Captain, wrapping his arms around his neck and hugging him."

"Oh, Joseph, what happened to you?"

"I was marooned here, once Jacky realized that I no longer had the map, he decided I should guard the treasure."

"You know where it is?" Captain asked, prying Joseph away from him.

"Of course not! Jacky may have been cruel, but not dumb."

They continued talking and completely ignored me. "Ahem," I coughed.

Captain spun around and seemed to realize I was standing there for the first time.

He smiled at me, "Robin," he said, taking Joseph by the shoulders and pushing him up beside him, "This is Joseph Key, known to many as the Key Thief."

"No, it can't be. My father is dead, dead! He abandoned me and now he is dead!"

A tear slid down Joseph's filthy face, leaving a streak. "I did not mean to abandon you, my beloved Robin, I only meant to protect you. Ol' Jacky would have killed you on the spot if he had known you were my child. That's why I left you for Barty to find. I was going to come back for you, but..." His voice faded away. "You have to believe me. I, I can't continue with out you. The only reason I am alive today is because I didn't give up on seeing you again. Please forgive me."

"I, I think I believe you." I walked up to him and hugged him. His arms closed around me and we hugged for the first time in sixteen years.

"I am so sorry," My father sobbed.

"Don't be. We are together now."

"And now I will never let you go."

I pushed away from him, "Oh, yes you will. Most of Captain's men smell better than you do, and I didn't think anything could smell worse than that!" Captain and I laughed while Joseph frowned and looked down at himself.

"Come on, Joseph, I have never said this to any of my men before, but you need a bath and a change of clothes."

Captain led Joseph away to a room on the eastern wall where warm water was being heated. His old clothes were thrown away and replaced with newer ones. He looked so much better with all of the dirt and grub washed off of him. I took the liberty of cutting off most of his wild hair. It came down to his ears when we could brush it all. His hair was washed again and when he was done, he looked like a new man. His eyes seemed brighter; more of a shade of blue, and his hair was now a light, sun bleached shade of brown. When I saw him "completed", as Captain said, I ran and hugged him.

"It feels so good to have a father." I cried in his arms.

"Yes, too bad it has to be at a time of war when I find you."

"Huh?"

"Captain has decided that I will fight, while you are to stay put in the fort." He got up and started walking away.

"But I fought when they came to my rescue on Henry's ship!" I cried after him.

"Yes, Barty told me that," he said, turning towards me and looking very disappointed. "That was a foolish decision, handing yourself over like that."

"But I fought you and won! I also succeeded in fighting on Henry's ship!"

"And nearly got yourself killed when you fought him!"

"But I-."

"I am sorry Robin, but you are staying here."

I sighed; devastated that I could not help them fight. "Is this what having a father feels like?"

He looked at me sternly, and then laughed. "You're just like your mother you know, completely stubborn, and yet so convincing, and beautiful," Hh added. I smiled at him while he held me in his arms again.

"So, how is your family? Dallas and Jody, are they well?"

"As far as I know they are."

"And Kent, how is he? He was three when I last saw him."

"He is nineteen now. He sails under Henry though."

"I believe I had another nephew, what was his name?"

"You had two other nephews. Timothy was seventeen and Zachery is eight."

"Ah, yes. And how are they?"

"I think Zachery is ok, but Timothy..." My voice trailed off. "He died just the other day."

"Oh, I am sorry, Robin. I had no idea."

"You couldn't have known."

"Any other family members?" he asked.

"Not that I know of."

He seemed relieved. I wondered if I did actually have any family members, if I did, he wasn't hinting on it.

11

THE DAGGER'S MARK

The sun sank with the tide. All of our men were lined up at the river, waiting for Captain's orders to cross. Since there was only one safe bridge, it looked like we would be getting a little wet. My instructions were clear. I was to help the others cross the river and then hide in the brush to help any retreating men cross back again. Yeah, right. My sword waited under a bush at the top of the hill, just as Father and I planned. I would meet with him on the battle field and fight beside him. I just had to help the men cross.

Someone bumped into me, nearly sending me down the steep incline and sprawling into the cold river water. "Watch it!" I whispered to him. My eyes lit up when I saw Sasha. He was mumbling an apology when I grabbed him by the shoulder and dragged him up the hill.

"You're a stubborn one aren't ya?" I questioned as loud as I dared.

"Oh, yeah?" he asked, squirming in my grip.

"Yeah! And you know what else?" He turned his face away from me. "You need to be that way to have a friend like me." I relaxed my grip on his shoulders and his feet returned to the ground. "Sorry about the other day, Sasha it's just that I-."

"I am the one that should be sorry. I over reacted, that's all. I mean, he was your cousin."

"Thanks for understanding. Now, didn't Captain tell you to stay put in the fort?"

Sasha looked down at his bare feet, looking embarrassed that he had been caught.

"It's not safe for you to wander around on a night like tonight." I paused, looking for a reaction that did not come. "It's not safe for you to wander around on a night like tonight," I repeated, "Without me." His face lit up in a huge smile. "Now you wait up there by that bush, yeah that one. I will be there in a moment to help you cross." I turned to leave but he caught me by the shoulder.

"Wait, I have something for you." He reached inside his pocket and pulled out something on a chain. "This is for you." He said, holding up a little charm on a golden chain. A red ruby sat inside a small carved piece of wood. "And that's not all," he continued, not waiting for me to ask questions or to say thank you, "I carved the wood and worked double time for Felix for the jewel."

"This is what you were trying to steal that one day!"

"And the chain," he continued, "The chain is the best part. Timothy gave me that chain to give to you."

"Timothy?"

"Now get out there. Look, Captain is giving the order!" I turned to look and when I looked back, Sasha had disappeared into the shadows. I hung the necklace around my neck and got back into position. Captain gave the signal, and we all slipped into the cold river.

The water was waist deep, so the men needed little help crossing the river, although Gunner did slip and fall. He splashed around in the water, screaming "Help! Help!" Captain grabbed him by his vest and hauled him up to his feet. Once he was on firm ground again, Captain slapped him across the face.

"You'll have his entire crew down on us!" he hissed. Our spy met us on the other side. Captain and Bengt, our spy, went over to the side to speak privately. Lucky for me, I had just dove back into the water. I slipped over to them and listened in on their "secret" conversation.

"We have too few men, Captain! They outnumber us nearly three to one!"

"Well, that won't be a problem." Captain shrugged. Bengt looked shocked.

"Sir?"

"It's simple really. If each of us kills three men, then there won't be much left. The average man usually kills more than that in a regular fight."

"Which means Henry's men can also kill that many." Bengt insisted.

"I said regular. Sure they are regular, but we are above that."

"What if one of us dies? Who will pick up the remainders?" he asked through gritted teeth.

"You ask too many questions. Now, let's go!" He said, waving his hand and signaling the men. He then turned to me, in the water, and said, "Get back to the fort, Robin." I was shocked that he had known I was there and had not said anything. He ran off before I could ask any questions. I waited until I could no longer see any of the men before swimming back across the river.

I fetched my sword along with Sasha and made my way back to the river. With Sasha on my back and my sword in my hand, I crossed the river for the third time, and hopefully not the last.

Gun shots sounded through the air. You could hear the clanging of blood thirsty swords and the cries of dying men as we drew closer. Smoke filled the air as some of the buildings of Fort Zarr burned. The sky seemed to turn red over the battle field.

"Stay to the shadows, Sasha. I don't want to lose you." Not giving him a chance to argue, I ran into the middle of a life changing battle. One man at a time fell to the ground as my sword cut through them. I looked around for anybody I knew, but they always seemed to be across the battle field.

"Robin! This is no place for a girl!" Kota called to me as he ran past me and away from one of Henry's giants.

"Robin what on earth are you doing here? Go back to the fort!" called another. Several more calls followed. I didn't bother to do what they said. I was looking for Henry. I was going to make him pay for what he did to Timothy.

Soon my total crept up to four downed men.

A hand grabbed my shoulder and dragged me off the battle field and into a nearby bush. I struggled to free my self from his iron grip but did not succeed. He pulled me down to my knees. I was spun around and came face to face with Kent.

"Robin, Henry has told me to find you and bring you to him. You need to come with me."

"What? No, I am not going with you!"

"Why not? Do you not want to be rescued?"

"I don't need to be rescued, especially not by Henry."

"Play along now, Robin, he has also told me to find Timothy and bring him also."

I was about to say a rather rude and un-lady like thing about Henry when I comprehended what Kent just said. "That might be hard to do."

"What do you mean? He is my brother after all. I want to help him."

"That's not what I mean." I was not sure if I should continue, but now I could not get out of saying it. "He, Henry did not tell you?"

"Tell me what?" I looked away from him, but he pulled me back to him, "Tell me what, Robin, tell me what?" He said, shaking me by my shoulders.

"Kent! Timothy is dead." He stopped shaking me and dropped me.

"No, the pirates took him captive, along with you!"

"Kent, Henry killed him. I watched him. Timothy is dead."

"Henry said that he thought Tim joined those monsters," he growled. He looked lost in thought so I tried to look for an escape route. "It must have been them!" He said, coming to his decision. "Those filthy beasts killed him!"

Another hand pulled me away from Kent, helping me up to my feet. "You ok, Robin?" my father asked me.

"Just fine, this is my cousin Kent." I said, pointing to Kent, who was still sitting on the ground.

"Young Master Kent, boy have you ever grown. Now Robin," he said, turning to me, "I thought you were staying close to me after they all crossed the river and I-."

"Excuse me," Kent interrupted, standing up, "Who are you?"

"Your uncle!" Joseph said cheerfully as he pulled me back into the battle. Father said he had to tend to something, so I looked around for Captain.

"Robin!" Captain called to me, "Where is your father?"

"He had to tend to something, I think he went that way," I said, pointing in the way my father went.

"Oh boy..." Captain's voice faded away. I turned to see what he was looking at and my gaze landed on my father, fighting with Henry. Captain pulled out his pistol, cocked it, and pointed it at the fighting men.

"No!" I shouted, pushing Captain's arm out of the way. The shot went off and one of Henry's men, sneaking up on us from the side, fell to the ground dead. "You could hit Da!" I started running to the dueling pair. Father had the upper hand, but I knew that could change in a matter of seconds.

Me and my big mouth.

Henry's sword cut across my father's middle. It wasn't a deep cut, nor did it look life threatening, but it diffidently looked painful. He dropped his sword in order to grasp his new wound.

"Father!" I called to him, running to his rescue. Henry sliced again, and this time, father fell to his knees. "No!" I screamed. Henry looked up at me and smiled. He picked up Father's sword and put the tip of it on father's chest and ever so slowly pushed it into him. I tripped over the sand and fell, getting a mouth full of it. Joseph fell to his side, unable to roll over to his back. When I stood up, Captain grabbed me from behind, trapping me in his powerful arms. He lifted me in the air and I thrashed around with my legs. "Let... Me... Go!" I wheezed. I looked back at Henry, who was wiping the blood from his sword on his handkerchief. He backed away slowly, and then disappeared into some brush and trees that stood alone on the sand.

Captain dropped me and I ran to my father's side.

"No!" I cried over top of him. I knew pulling the sword out of his chest would just cause more bleeding so I sat there beside him, helpless. "Captain." I cried. He dropped to his knees beside him. Kody looked shocked as he ran passed us, but it was Kota who ripped off his shirt and gave it to Captain. He then covered our position from behind while Captain ripped the shirt into smaller, bandage like pieces.

"No," Father wheezed. He turned to me and said, "The treasure lies in the heart... Watch... Watch out for..." His head rolled backward, and his outstretched hand dropped. My head dropped, but my gaze lifted to see Henry running away into the rising sun. A thousand thoughts raced through my head. My anger grew and I gritted my teeth. I shot up and ran at Henry.

"Murderer!" I screamed at him as I chased after him.

"Robin, wait!" Captain called after me. I did not listen to him. I raced through the sand, stumbling at times, and falling at others. I chased him up the path to the treasure, around the pit trap. It was there that I lost him. I stood at the path and screamed for him to come back and fight. I dropped to the ground and sobbed.

What had father said? 'The treasure lies at the heart...' The heart of what? Was it a metaphor, or... I jumped to my feet and ran up the path. Directions! My father's last words had been directions to the treasure! *The heart of what?* I thought again. *The mountain.* I looked up, but did not see anything from under the dense canopy of the jungle. I charged up the rest of the path, past the swinging logs, and over the bridge. I passed numberless pits and traps. I had no time to look at my feet so I hoped I would not fall into one of the traps set along this path. Most of the traps looked like they had been sprung, either recently or many long years ago.

I could see Henry in the distance. He looked back at me, and then ducked into a bush. Surely he wasn't hiding in such a pitiful hiding place as that. I approached the bush cautiously, my sword leading the way. I used my sword to move the bush away and was surprised to see a hole in the rocky wall behind the bush. I got down on my hands and knees and crawled through the opening. It was a long tunnel, so I hoped Henry was not waiting for me on the other side. What I saw on the other side of the tunnel, inside of that cave, I will do well not to forget.

The floor was covered with water, like a small lake. The depth of the pool ranged from spots that were only ankle deep, like around the edges, and other spots appeared to be knee deep. A little island sat in the middle of the surprisingly well lit room. A palm tree grew on the sandy piece of land. I looked up at the beam of sunlight streaming down through the ceiling, landing on the island. Henry was standing in knee deep water, staring at the map in his hands.

"Ah, Robin," he said, turning to me, "It is so good to see you again, my dearly beloved." Why was he doing this? Didn't he try to kill me last time we met? I couldn't understand what he wanted so I asked him.

"What do you want, Henry?"

His laugh echoed through the cave. I heard the bush rattling in the distance and I hoped Henry didn't have any more goons coming after me.

"What do I want? You came to me, Sweetness, so the real question is what do you want? Are you finally accepting my proposal?"

"Never."

"Well then what do you want?" he asked, looking rather irritated.

"I want you to pay," I said through gritted teeth. I spit the rest of the sand out of my mouth. He smiled a petty smile at me before looking down again at the map. "Why are you doing this, Henry? You have never been interested in treasure before. You are rich enough as it is!"

"Ah, yes, but wouldn't it look great if I gave it all to your poor, dying family?"

"What are you talking about?" I asked, suddenly cautious.

"Well isn't it obvious? Your cousin, never mind his name, is dead. Zachery, well, nobody cares about him, and Kent... I won't need him any more. Once he brings me what I need, I think you will be more willing."

"I will let you go now, Henry, if you just drop your sword..." I let my voice trail off. *Yes, drop your sword. And as soon as you do, I'll tie you up faster than...*

His laughter filled the cave again, "Oh, Robin, to gamble like that you need to have all the cards." He waved his hand at someone behind me and Kent, along with Baldy and another man who had a huge scar across his face, walked past me into the room. That wasn't the least of my worries. Kent and Baldy were holding Sasha by his wrists.

"How did you-."

126

"Oh it was easy to find him," Henry bragged, "After all, he stayed in the shadows just like you asked." He must have noticed my surprised face because he added, "Yes, I heard your conversation and I have to admit, it was very tempting to just grab you there. But I want more than that. I want you to agree to marry me, not to be forced. I knew that threatening your life wouldn't help, so I thought I would threaten someone else's life."

He waved again to the men, and Kent dropped Sasha's hand and went to stand by Henry. Baldy twisted Sasha's arm behind him and held a knife to his throat. Scar face came behind me and grabbed my wrist. "So what will it be, Robin? Will you marry me? Or will you let this poor misfortunate soul die?"

I remained silent, grinding my teeth so hard, it hurt. "Hmm, pity." Henry shrugged. He raised his hand up and Baldy drew the knife back and brought it towards Sasha's chest.

I squeezed my eyes shut and turned away. "Fine, I'll marry you." The blade stopped and Baldy released Sasha. He fell to the water with a splash. Scar face pushed me towards Henry. I heard a faint whizzing sound. Scar face tensed and fell into the water. His back side floated to the surface and a little green feathered dart stuck out from his back.

"What the..." Henry began and before he could finish, Captain and Nkunda burst into the room, swords

127

drawn. Captain immediately went after Baldy, and Nkunda engaged Kent, leaving me to deal with Henry.

"Are you ready?" I asked him, sword up and prepared.

"As ready as I'll ever be." He drew his sword along with a little dagger from his pocket. He attacked first. I dodged his dagger and reached for his leg. He blocked it and pushed me back. Again he attacked with his dagger and I dodged. I attempted a shot aimed for his shoulder this time, but again he blocked it with his sword. He pushed me back again, but this time he kept pushing. He kept me in retreat and pushed me around the lake like I was little more than a child. I started to get tired. A sharp pain in my side formed, but I kept fighting back.

I noticed that Henry was only using his sword now. Had he dropped the dagger? Or had he only put it up to prove that he was my better and could beat me without it? It didn't matter. Henry stumbled in the water and I took that time to look around the cave. Nkunda had Kent tied to the tree and was sneaking up on Henry from behind and Captain was finishing up on Baldy. Baldy no longer had his sword and he held his hands in the air. He was talking to Captain. Captain pointed his sword to the tunnel and Baldy fled down it.

Henry was up again. I was tired. I threw my sword arm out in a jab and was surprised to see it catch his shoulder. He yelped in pain and surprise and dropped the sword he carried. We were both breathing heavily and when I started walking towards him, sword pointing at him, he fell. He crawled away, still facing me, and got himself stuck in a corner. I pointed my sword at him. Nkunda joined me on my left and Caption on my right.

"Now," I began, "You killed my father." Henry tried to disappear into the wall behind him. He kept pushing himself backwards.

"Now, now, Robin, I didn't know he was your father!"

"I had one for one night! You killed him and Timothy!"

"But think of all of the men you killed!" I raised my sword to his throat. "No, no need to be hasty." Henry pleaded with me. He kept looking me up and down, expecting me to drop dead. We all shifted backwards uneasily when Henry suddenly revealed his sword from beneath the water. His gaze rested on me before he spoke again... "I see my handy work is taking its toll. Now people will tell of how I tragically died, trying to save your life!" He took up his sword, blade facing down, and shoved it into his chest. He fell into the water as a red cloud spread out around his floating body. I was shocked. I stood there stunned, watching his dead body float in the water.

I turned to Captain, "What just happened?" I asked him.

"He took the cowards' way out. I don't know what he was yammering about though. He might have just..." Captain stopped mid sentence. He kneeled down in front of me and looked at something on my shirt. He lifted me off my feet and took me to the island and made me lay down.

"Captain, what's wrong?" I asked him, completely confused. The pain in my side was growing stronger.

"Don't move," he said. He took off his coat, then his white tunic and began ripping it into strips.

"What are you doing?"

"Fixing Henry's 'handiwork'." I looked down at my side and gasped. The pain grew stronger. Protruding from my side was the hilt of Henry's dagger. "It's not in deep so it won't be hard to pull out. Robin, calm yourself, you're panting like a dog."

"There is a knife in my side! What do you expect me to do?" I shrieked. I started to feel light headed. My breathing rate increased even more.

"Robin, look at me. That's it. Now I want you to breathe in... and out... in... and out... in... and..." He yanked the handle of the dagger out of my side. "Out," he said cheerfully. I screamed in pain, watching in horror as blood poured out of the gap.

"This fresh water, Captain." Nkunda called to us. "Wash out the wound with it."

Captain dipped one of the strips into the cool water and gently patted the cut. "Stay with us, Robin, stay with us." He mumbled. He kept mumbling about promising someone's father about watching over his little girl but I wasn't listening, I was barely alive. My vision became fuzzy around the edges after a while and I began to feel light headed again. "It won't stop bleeding!" Captain shouted at Nkunda.

They shouted at each other on what to do with the cut when another figure approached me. He kneeled next to me and checked over my wound. He put something in his mouth and chewed it up. He then applied what ever it was he put in his mouth to my cut. It was completely gross and unsanitary but I was defenseless. After a minute, the pain began to ease.

"Sleep tight, little girl," said a voice that I did not recognize. I sighed and rested my head on the ground. I could feel myself being lifted from the ground and carried out of the cave. I bumped along until we reached the ship. Then I was loaded onto a small boat and taken back to the ship. It wasn't until I was laid out in the mess hall that I finally slept.

12

CAPTAIN'S STORY

My eyes cracked open and I looked around the room. Sunlight streaked in through the cracks and crevices in the wall. I sat up slowly and placed my bare feet on the cold, wooden floor. The first thing I realized was that my side hurt. I pulled my shirt up and found bandages wrapped around my middle. I was sitting on a hammock, below deck. I stood and took slow, careful steps up onto the main deck. Men bustled around the deck. I was greeted by warm and cheerful smiles everywhere I looked. Some people on board I did not recognize. The sun gave me the energy I needed to begin my search for Captain.

"Quarter Master!" I called to Felix as he rushed by. He seemed to be the only person who did not great me with a smile.

"What do you want? I am in the middle of something." He continued on in his hurried pace so I walked towards Nkunda instead.

"Nkunda!"

"Ah, Robin. You up and moving again!"

"Do you know where Captain is?" I asked him.

"Yes," He said, continuing on with the task at hand.

"Aren't you going to tell me?"

"Tell you what?"

"Tell me where Captain is?"

"Oh! He in his room."

"Thank you, and one more thing."

"Yes?" he asked impatiently.

"How many men did we lose?"

Nkunda froze mid stride. He sighed and turned to face me slowly, "It's not good to dwell on past."

"It's just a number, Nkunda."

"Too many," Nkunda said before hurrying off.

I didn't want to pester him any longer, so I headed towards Captain's quarters. I wanted more information than that. I also wanted to know why I couldn't remember who won the battle.

"Captain!" I called as I entered the room.

"Hmm?" He said, too engrossed in whatever was on his desk to even bother looking up at me.

"I have questions that don't have answers."

He finally looked up and realized to whom he was speaking, "Robin, my girl! It's good to see you on your feet again!"

"Aye, Sir. I was just curious about the battle and what happened. I can't seem to remember anything but being in the cave with you."

"Well that's an easy question! We won. When Tanner ran back to the battle and announced Henry's death, they all dropped their swords and took cover in the bushes. It took us ages to fish them all out."

"But who is Tanner?"

"Tanner, you know, big guy, bald, skimpy little beard that looks like a spike."

"Oh yeah, I spared him back on *The Vengeance*," I shrugged.

"And that's a good thing too. He's to whom you owe your thanks."

"What do you mean?"

"He put something in your side there and carried you all the way back to the ship. He tried to swim to the ship, but decided you better go over in the cutter."

"Can you see that he gets part of the treasure once we find it?"

"I have already given him his portion."

"Gave him his what?"

"Just his share of the treasure."

"But we don't have the treasure!"

"Yes we do. You found it!"

"Must I ask what again?"

His laughter filled the room. I looked down at what he was preoccupied with before I entered the room and I am sure my jaw dropped when I saw it. The biggest ruby I had ever seen was lying on his desk. He must have noticed my disappointment because he said, "What's wrong?"

"I didn't find it. I lost. I didn't complete my task."

"Yes you did, you found it!"

"I was half dead! How could I have found it?"

"You were laying on it, Robin."

"I was what?"

Captain pulled something out of his pocket and tossed it to me. I snatched it out of the air and turned it over in my hand, studying the small, blue gem.

"That, my dear, was stuck in your back. When Tanner was taking you back to the ship, it fell off of you."

I was enticed by this beautiful object. "What kind is it?"

"That is a sapphire. There is plenty more where that came from. Would you like to see the treasure?"

"Would I ever!"

"I will take you there as soon as we discuss one last point."

"Aye, Sir?" I asked, already on my way to the door.

"Sit down, Robin."

I was not sure where this was heading, so I sat down across from him. "Is there a problem?"

"No, no, I just wanted to speak with you about an important matter."

"And that is?" I asked, eager to see the treasure.

"Robin, as you know your father has recently passed..." His voice trailed off. My eagerness faded and I sunk into the chair. "I promised your father that I would look after you if he failed his task. Seeing that he just died, I feel it is important to complete my part of the deal so I wanted to ask you a very important question."

I looked up at his weathered, tan face and our eyes locked. I did it. I found out what I was missing when our eyes locked those many weeks ago. Love. There was love in his eyes, but not the kind of love that I had thought. He wasn't in love, he was searching for it.

"Robin, many years ago I had a wife. Her name was Veronica. I loved her to the end of the world, but she died in child birth. The baby, she didn't make it either. I swore to myself that day that I would never love another as much as them ever again, but I lied. Once I discovered *The Cosmar* in our family heritage, I fell in love with it, along with the crew and the sea. But something, or rather, someone was missing.

"Robin, you know that I treat everyone on this ship as family so you know that I had all of the sons I could ever possibly want. But I was missing a piece. I was missing a daughter, and I found her. Robin, not only do I want you to be part of my crew, but I..." his voice trailed off.

"You what?" I urged him. I was almost in tears listening to his life story and he couldn't stop now. I needed to know where I came into this.

"I want to adopt you, Robin, but only if you allow it," he added quickly.

"You, adopt me?"

"Only if you want to. I know what it is like, not having a father for so many years and then when you find him, you lose him. I have been there. It happened to me. I just want you to know that there are others that love you too."

I sat there, unable to move, unable to breath. I then catapulted myself over the desk and into his loving arms. His laughter filled the room again as the chair he sat in tipped over and we fell to the ground. I was too happy to care about the pain the leap brought.

"Now run along. We will go see the treasure in a moment. Go and get some fresh air."

"Will do, Sir." I walked out of the room when I saw Carlos, or rather he saw me.

"Robin!"

"Carlos?" he ran over to me.

"Are you okay? Mr. Captain Sir said that you got hit pretty badly. You were out for three days!"

"Nothing that I can't handle. Just wait until you hear the news!"

137

"News... Which news?"

"That Captain adopted me!"

"Oh yes! That news! Congratulations, Chica!"

"But, he just told me... How could you have known?"

"This is a ship, Chica. News-."

"Yes, yes. News gets around to everyone. He is taking me to see the treasure, soon I hope."

"Well good luck, Chica. I have some work to finish up here."

Kody was the next person I spotted, although I didn't see him until he was right in front of me.

"Watch yourself, Robin, or you'll be fallin' overboard."

"Sorry Kody. Say, I haven't seen Kota today. Have you seen him?"

The joy on Kody's face vanished instantly. You wouldn't have noticed it unless you were watching him. "Is something wrong?" I asked him. He refused to look at me. "Kody what is it, what's wrong!" He slowly turned my way but still did not look at me.

"It's Kota. He was... he was injured in the battle. He... he didn't..." His voice broke off into crying.

"Kody!" I shouted at him, shaking him back to his senses. "What didn't he do?"

"His arm... I don't think he will make it." He said between sobs.

"Where is he?"

"All the injured stayed back at the fort." Kody pointed at the fort without looking at it. I leaned up against the rail, looking for the cutter. I finally spotted it at shore. Three people were hopping out of it. I looked down at the water, and then back up at the beach. It wasn't too far, but I was worried how well I could swim with this hole in my side.

I ignored my fears and pulled myself up and over the railing, sending me falling into the water below. I popped up to the surface, crying out at the pain the salt water made when it interacted with my cuts. I started towards the beach, cautious about coral reefs and fish in these waters.

I didn't care about the shouts that came from the ship as I swam towards the beach. It didn't take long before I was walking through waist deep water, and then knee deep, ankle deep, and then I was burning my feet on the hot sand as I ran to the fort.

I held my side as I approached the fort. A single guard sat watch at the entrance to the fort. I asked him where the injured were and he pointed out two different buildings in which to search. The first building I checked was fairly empty, with only two men lying on stretchers.

The second building was the exact opposite. It had eight men, either lying on the floor or on crudely made benches. I found Kota there. He was in the far corner so I had to step over several moaning men to reach him. Kota was propped up against the wall; a

139

blanket covered his right side. He smiled at me when I approached.

"I see you woke up," Kota said.

"It took me a while but yes, I am awake."

Kota stared at me hard before exclaiming, "You're wet." I looked down at my dripping clothes and I had to laugh.

"How are you?" I asked him.

He seemed to think about the question before replying, "Spectacular."

"Kody was on the ship, mumbling about you being hurt and that you didn't do something. Since our talk was not very productive, I swam here to find you, although my side is killing me."

"That's why you're wet!" Kota exclaimed, happy to have figured out the mystery.

"So, where did you get hit? From what Kody said, it sounded pretty... good gracious!" I exclaimed when Kota pulled off the blanket.

"My arm was cut severely in the fight. Nkunda said I wouldn't last unless it was cut off." I kneeled next to him on his little raised bed. I touched the clean bandages that were wrapped tightly around his shoulder.

"How will you fight?"

Kota looked away. Apparently he had thought about this before. He looked back at me. "I will make it work. This injury is not going to stop me from doing the things I love. I will find a way; maybe even use my left arm in the next raid."

"That's one thing I always admired about you, Kota. You never stopped going."

"What about you? You were nearly killed three days ago and you are already up on your feet again! I mean seriously, you just swam over from the ship just to check on me. I had to get my skills from somebody now didn't I?"

"You are too modest."

"I hate to be rude, but I could really use a rest. Think you could send Kody down when you see him?"

"I will try to remember."

"Be careful, Robin. There are some men that were not found on the island."

"Really?"

"They were probably killed and lost, but you never know. Keep your guard up and you will be fine." I turned and began exiting the room, taking one careful step after the other. I heard a moan from underneath me and lifted my foot. I had stepped on someone's hand.

"Oh, sorry, Sir! I didn't mean it, honest! I was just-. Sasha?" I dropped down beside him and held his hand. "Sasha what happened?" Another moan escaped him. His head was bandaged and his hair stuck through it in spots.

"Hit his head pretty good, he did. Got quite a bump there. He will wake soon." I turned around and saw Tanner.

"You're helping here?"

"I suggested that the wounded be kept here. Don't think badly of me, Robin. I was not going to kill him. I would never harm a hair on any of Robin's friends."

"Why not? Were you not part of *The Vengeance?*"

"My head was there but my heart was with my peoples customs. I owed you. You spared me, Robin, one does not forget that easily. I would have left with you, but I was still loyal to Henry then."

"That's why you dropped Sasha so suddenly."

"I did not give him that bump though. I am afraid Scot and Kent ruffed him up before they brought him to Henry. I tried to stop them, but then they would know that I didn't want to help them anymore."

"You did well. He might not have survived if Scar Face or Kent was holding him."

"We lost many men; a child was not worth losing."

"How many died?" Another moan came from Sasha.

"Let's see... 50 men were on *The Vengeance* and 35 on *The Cosmar*... Eight men were killed from *The Cosmar*... 20 from *The Vengeance*. Fifteen of *The*

142

Vengeance decided to join *The Cosmar's* crew while the rest wanted to stay on the island."

"You mean fifteen men wanted to stay on the island? They will starve without enough resources! They won't survive!"

"Actually only ten men chose to stay. The other five are missing."

"And those five are?"

"Scot, or Scar face as you called him." I blushed when he called him by the nickname I had given the man. "A few others whose names have escaped me. And Kent, whom I have recently been informed was your cousin."

"Kent disappeared?"

"Aye, right after Henry was killed."

"But you didn't see Henry die. You left before that and told every one else that he was dead... Why?"

"I saw him stick you with his knife before I left. I knew what he had in mind so I sped the process up some. I told everyone that he was dead and then went and searched for the herb I applied to your wound, which reminds me. That bandage is old. It needs to be changed."

Tanner took me to the upper room of the building, said I needed some privacy or something, and changed my bandages there. He applied some sort of cold liquid that took away the pain in my side immediately.

"Can you apply this stuff to the others too?"

"Trust me when I say that I would give it to all. There are some restrictions to using Samara though. It's very tricky. You have to apply this stuff to the wound first because it reacts differently with all kinds of substances so it's very risky."

"And you applied it to me even though it wasn't applied first?" I asked worriedly, looking down at my side.

"No worries. I applied Majesty to you first. It's a beautiful purple flower that grows in rare places. Only in the darkest parts of caves does it grow. You are lucky I found it because the Samara was still on *The Vengeance*.

"The other reason I haven't applied this to all is because Samara is only grown in The Icy North. Only the Lonely Tribes wander there."

"Well then how did you get it?"

"I said the Lonely Tribes wandered there didn't I?"

"You were part of the Lonely Tribe?"

"Aye, for a time I was. I haven't visited in over five years so my supply of Samara is running low."

"Thank you," I said as he finished up on the last bandage. I was afraid my cut would look as bad as Timothy's so I was relieved to see that I didn't have any green slimy gunk in there. No, the wound had started to close up, according to Tanner. I should be completely back up and running within a few days.

"Captain just landed, I believe he wants to talk to you."

"You just know everything, don't you, Tanner?"

"I know how to use my ears if that's what you mean. He is calling for you outside."

"Oh," I blushed.

"Run along. He wants to show you something."

"Thanks Tanner. Oh and before I leave I wanted to tell you that Captain adopted me."

"He told me he wanted to. I am glad you accepted."

"See you, Tanner. Watch over Sasha for me will you?" I ran over to the window and looked out. I put one foot out on to the balcony, and then the other. The support beams would be easy to slide down. As soon as I put pressure on my foot, it gave way, sending me sprawling and shrieking down the balcony, and straight into the arms of Captain.

"Be careful, Robin, or you will have us all in the sick bay with heart attacks!"

"Sorry, Sir."

"Come and walk with me. I want to show you the treasure."

"Ok!" I said eagerly as he set me down. We walked down the beach to where the path started.

"You shouldn't have jumped overboard, Robin. It was very dangerous seeing that we are in uncharted waters where coral reefs are waiting to cut your feet to shreds if you step on them."

"Sorry, Sir, I just had to check on Kota. Kody was mumbling something about him being severely hurt so I had to jump overboard to check on him."

"Just don't let it happen again." We walked in silence for a while. When we started on the trail, Captain asked, "How is your side doing? Considering that you jumped from the ship into salt water, and then jumped off of the roof, I am forced to believe that it is nearly healed."

"Tanner said I should be completely back up and running in a few days."

"I think he is underestimating your abilities. You look perfectly healthy to me."

"It hurts sometimes, but other than that, the only annoying thing is these itchy bandages."

"Well I know how that feels." Captain chuckled.

"Captain?"

"Yes?"

"Back on the ship, in your cabin, you said something about you know how I feel, right after you talked about me losing my dad. What did you mean?"

"I want you to know right now that I once had a family too. My mother always kept me and my father visited at times, but he always stayed at sea. On my twentieth birthday, Father decided that it was time that I learned 'The family trade' so he took me on a raid. We had a glorious time until he suffered a fatal wound. He died shortly after."

"I am sorry."

"It was many years ago, Robin. There is no need to dwell in the past, nor to look to far ahead at the future. It is best to keep your mind set on things that are happening right now."

"I miss him," I whispered

"I do too. Joseph was one of the best men I have ever had. You came here searching for the treasure, but you found something much more. Not all treasure is silver and gold."

"So what is our next endeavor?" I asked him.

"We need more supplies so I was thinking we would stop by Saint Ryan before we do anything else."

"Great! Somebody needs to tell my aunt and uncle about Timothy and Kent so it might as well be me. Plus I need to apologize for leaving and thank them for not letting me go with the Mackenzies or I might have never met you. And besides, they need to meet you too!"

"Yes, I suppose a greeting is in order."

"But one more thing."

"And that is?"

"If you are going to meet my aunt and uncle, you are going to need a bath." I started running up the trail. He stopped and looked ahead at me. He then smiled and took off after me, chasing me all the way to the treasure.

147

"For where

Your treasure is,

There will your heart be also."

Luke 12:34 NIV